# Marie de France
# Bisclavret: A Medieval Tale

## Original Text, Translation, and Word Lists

## Translated by
## Matthew Leigh Embleton

For a list of books by the author please visit:
www.matthewleighembleton.co.uk

# Marie de France - Bisclavret

Cover: An illustration of a werewolf on an imaginary medieval manuscript
Source: A.I. generated

# Acknowledgments

I have long been fascinated by languages and history, and I am very grateful to the special people in my life who have supported and encouraged me in my work. Thank you for believing in me. You know who you are.

# Introduction

Marie de France (fl 1160 to 1215) was a poet born in France who lived in England during the late 12th century. She was well known at the Plantagenet royal court of King Henry II of England and Eleanor of Aquitaine, and she is believed to have been an abbess of a monastery. Her poems or 'Lais' are believed to have been written sometime between 1160 and 1175 drawing upon Breton and Arthurian myths and legends.

It is written in a form of Old French known as 'Anglo-Norman', which came from 'Old Norman', part of the 'Langues d'oïl' dialect continuum of Gallo-Romance languages. Old French is the result of a gradual separation from Vulgar Latin and Common Romance, coming into contact with influences from Gaulish (Continental Celtic), and Frankish (Germanic).

The text is presented in the original Old French, with a literal word-for-word line-by-line translation, and a Modern English translation, all side-by-side. In this way, it is possible to see and feel how Old French worked and how it has evolved.

Also included is a word list with 1,318 Old French words translated in to English, and 1,271 English words translated into Old French.

This book is designed to be of use and interest to anyone with a passion for the Old French language, French history, or languages and history in general.

# Marie de France - Bisclavret

| | *Old French* | Literal | English |
|---|---|---|---|
| 1 | Quant des lais faire m'entremet, | When of-them lays do I-begin, | When I begin (to compose) lays, |
| 2 | ne vueil ubliër Bisclavret. | not I-wish forget Bisclavret. | I do not wish to forget Bisclavret. |
| 3 | Bisclavret a nun en Bretan, | Bisclavret has the-name in Breton, | His name is Bisclavret in Breton, |
| 4 | Garulf l'apelent li Norman. | Garulf they-call the Normans. | The Normans call him Garulf. |
| 5 | Jadis le poeit hum oïr | Days-passed one could him hear | In days passed one could hear him, |
| 6 | e sovent suleit avenir, | and time-to-time used frequently, | and this used to happen frequently, |
| 7 | hume plusur garulf devindrent | man many Garulf became | many a man became a werewolf |
| 8 | e es boscages maisun tindrent. | and in-those woods house had. | and made his house in the woods. |
| 9 | Garulf, ceo est beste salvage; | Garulf, behold-this is beast savage; | Werewolf, that is a wild animal; |
| 10 | tant cum il est en cele rage, | as-much with it is in this rage, | as long as he is in this rage, |
| 11 | humes devure, grant mal fait; | men devours, great harm does; | He devours men, and does great harm; |
| 12 | es granz forez converse e vait. | in-those grand forests about and goes. | In the grand forests he goes about. |
| 13 | Cest afaire les ore ester; | This matter let now stand; | This matter now I let be; |
| 14 | del Bisclavret vus vueil cunter. | of-this Bisclavret you I-want to-recount. | I want to tell you about Bisclavret. |
| 15 | En Bretaigne maneit uns ber, | In Brittany lived one baron, | In Brittany there lived a baron, |
| 16 | merveille l'ai oï loër. | marvellously of-him I-hear praise. | of whom I hear marvellous praise. |
| 17 | Beals chevaliers e bons esteit | Handsome knight and good he-was | A handsome and good knight he was, |
| 18 | e noblement se cunteneit. | and nobly he led-himself. | And nobly he led himself. |

4

| | Old French | Literal | English |
|---|---|---|---|
| 19 | De sun seignur esteit privez | Of his lord he-was close | Of his lord he was a close friend, |
| 20 | e de tuz ses veisins amez. | and of all his neighbours loved. | and by all his neighbours he was loved. |
| 21 | Femme ot espuse mult vaillant | Woman had wife much valiant | He had a woman as his wife who was much valiant, |
| 22 | e ki mult faiseit bel semblant. | and of much made beautiful appearance. | and who was beautiful in appearance. |
| 23 | Il amot li e ele lui; | He loved her and she him; | He loved her, and she loved him; |
| 24 | mes d'une chose ert grant ennui, | but of-one thing was great grief, | but one thing caused her great grief, |
| 25 | qu'en la semeine le perdeit | that-in the week him lost | that in the week she lost him, |
| 26 | treis jurs entiers qu'el ne saveit | three days entire with not knowing | for three days without knowing, |
| 27 | que deveneit ne u alout, | what became nor where went, | what became of him nor where he went, |
| 28 | ne nuls des soens niënt n'en sout. | nor none of his nothing about knew. | and none of his people knew about it. |
| 29 | Une feiz esteit repairiez | One time was-he returned | Once he returned |
| 30 | a sa maisun joius e liez; | to his home joyous and happy; | to his home joyous and happy; |
| 31 | demandé li a e enquis. | asked she to and inquired. | she asked and inquired. |
| 32 | Sire', fait el, bealz, dulz amis, | 'My-lord', said she, 'gentle, sweet friend, | 'My lord', she said, 'gentle and sweet friend, |
| 33 | une chose vus demandasse | one thing I-wish to-ask | one thing I wish to ask you |
| 34 | mult volentiers, se jeo osasse; | much willing, if I dare; | very much, if I dare; |
| 35 | mes jeo criem tant vostre curut | but I fear so-much your anger | but I fear your anger so much |
| 36 | que nule rien tant ne redut'. | that any nothing as-much nor dread'. | that there is nothing I dread so much'. |
| 37 | Quant il l'oï, si l'acola, | When he that-heard, so he-embraced, | When he heard that, he embraced her, |

| | Old French | Literal | English |
|---|---|---|---|
| 38 | *vers lui la traist, si la baisa.* | to him her drew-close, so her kissed. | drew her close to him, and kissed her. |
| 39 | *Dame', fait il, or demandez!* | 'Madam', said he, 'just ask! | 'Madam', he said, 'just ask! |
| 40 | *Ja cele chose ne querrez,* | Never such thing not ask, | Never such a thing will you ask, |
| 41 | *se jo la sai, ne la vus die'.* | of me that I-know, not the answer you. | of me that if I know, I will not answer you. |
| 42 | *Par fei', fet ele, or sui guarie!* | By faith, said she, 'now I-am relieved! | 'By my faith', she said, 'now I am relieved!' |
| 43 | *Sire, jeo sui en tel esfrei* | My-lord, I am in much fear | My lord, I am in such fear, |
| 44 | *les jurs quant vus partez de mei.* | the days when you part from me. | on the days when you take leave of me. |
| 45 | *El cuer en ai mult grant dolur* | In my-heart in have much great pain | In my heart I have such great pain, |
| 46 | *e de vus perdre tel poür,* | and of you loss such horror, | and such horror at the thought of losing you, |
| 47 | *se jeo nen ai hastif cunfort,* | if I do-not have swift comfort, | that if I do not have swift comfort, |
| 48 | *bien tost en puis aveir la mort.* | well quickly and then have of death. | then I may well die soon. |
| 49 | *Kar me dites u vus alez,* | Come me tell where you go, | Come now, tell me where you go, |
| 50 | *u vus estes e conversez!* | where you are and about! | where you are, and where you dwell! |
| 51 | *Mun esciënt que vus amez,* | To-me it-seems that you-have a-love, | It seems to me as though you have a sweetheart, |
| 52 | *e se si est, vus meserrez'.* | and if so are, you misguided'. | and if so, you are misguided'. |
| 53 | *Dame', fet il, pur deu merci!* | 'Madam', said he, by god's mercy! | 'Madam', he said, 'by god's mercy! |
| 54 | *Mals m'en vendra, se jol vus di;* | Bad to-me comes, if I you tell; | Bad will come to me, if I tell you; |
| 55 | *kar de m'amur vus partirai* | therefore of my-love yours will-part | therefore my love will part, |
| 56 | *e mei meïsmes en perdrai'.* | and me myself then destroy. | and then me myself will be destroyed. |

| | Old French | Literal | English |
|---|---|---|---|
| 57 | Quant la dame l'a entendu, | When the lady this heard, | When the lady heard this, |
| 58 | ne l'a niënt en gab tenu. | nor that nothing in jest beheld. | she knew that it was not in jest. |
| 59 | Suventes feiz li demanda. | Repeatedly put she questions. | Repeatedly she asked him questions. |
| 60 | Tant le blandi e losenja | So-much him cajoled and praised | So she flattered and praised him, |
| 61 | que s'aventure li cunta; | that his-adventure he recounted; | that he told her of his adventure; |
| 62 | nule chose ne li cela. | any thing not was concealed. | and nothing did he conceal from her. |
| 63 | Dame, jeo deviene bisclavret. | Madam, I become Bisclavret. | Madam, I become a werewolf. |
| 64 | En cele grant forest me met | In that great forest I go | In that great forest I go, |
| 65 | al plus espés de la gualdine, | to most thick of the forest, | to the thickest part of the woods, |
| 66 | s'i vif de preie e de ravine'. | thus live by plunder and of theft. | and there I live by plunder and theft. |
| 67 | Quant il li aveit tut cunté, | When he her had all recounted, | When he had recounted everything to her, |
| 68 | enquis li a e demandé | queried she and of asked | she queried him and asked him |
| 69 | s'il se despueille u vet vestuz. | whether he unclothed or goes dressed. | whether he went clothed or unclothed. |
| 70 | Dame', fet il, jeo vois tuz nuz'. | Madam', said he, 'I go totally nude'. | Madam', he said, 'I go totally naked'. |
| 71 | Di mei pur deu u sunt voz dras!' | 'Tell me by god where are your clothes!' | 'Tell me by god where are your clothes!' |
| 72 | Dame, ceo ne dirai jeo pas; | 'Madam, this not will-tell I not; | 'Madam, this I do not want to tell you; |
| 73 | kar se jes eüsse perduz | because if I were to-lose | because if I were to lose them, |
| 74 | e de ceo fusse aparceüz, | and of that had-been aware, | and if I become aware (of losing them), |
| 75 | bisclavret sereie a tuz jurs. | Bisclavret I-would-be of all days. | I would be a werewolf for all days. |
| 76 | Ja nen avreie mes sucurs, | I not could me help, | No help could ever again avail me, |
| 77 | desi qu'il me fussent rendu. | until which to-me would-be returned. | until they would be returned to me. |

| Old French | Literal | English |
|---|---|---|
| 78 *Pur ceo ne vueil qu'il seit seü'.* | Therefore this not want which to-be known. | Therefore that is why I do not wish it to be known. |
| 79 *Sire', la dame li respunt,* | 'My-lord', the woman to-him responded, | 'My lord', the woman responded to him, |
| 80 *jeo vus eim plus que tut le mund.* | 'I you love more than all the world. | 'I love you more than all the world. |
| 81 *Nel me devez niënt celer* | Not me should nothing conceal | Nothing should you conceal from me, |
| 82 *ne mei de nule rien duter;* | nor mine of any nothing doubt; | Nor doubt my understanding of anything; |
| 83 *ne semblereit pas amistié,* | not would-look-like not friendship, | that would not look like friendship, |
| 84 *Qu'ai jeo forfait, pur quel pechié* | what-have I committed, by what sin | what have I committed, and by what sin |
| 85 *me dutez vus de nule rien?* | me doubt you of not nothing? | that you doubt me not of nothing? |
| 86 *Dites le mei! Si ferez bien'.* | Tell it to-me! So will-do well. | Tell me, so you will do well. |
| 87 *Tant l'anguissa, tant le suzprist,* | So anguish, such he under-pressed, | Such anguish, he was pressed, |
| 88 *ne pout el faire, si li dist.* | naught could he do, but her tell. | there was naught he could do but tell her. |
| 89 *Dame', fet il, de lez cel bois,* | 'Madam', said he, 'of near the forest, | Madam', he said, 'near the forest, |
| 90 *lez le chemin par unt jeo vois,* | near the path by then I go, | near the path I go by, |
| 91 *une viez chapele i estait,* | an old chapel is standing, | there stands an old chapel, |
| 92 *ki meinte feiz grant bien me fait.* | which many times great good me has-done. | which many times has done me well. |
| 93 *La est la piere cruese e lee* | There is the stone hollow and wide | There is a hollow and wide stone |
| 94 *suz un buissun, dedenz cavee.* | under a bush, inside dug-out. | under a bush, inside a dug-out. |
| 95 *Mes dras i met suz le buissun,* | My clothes I put under the bush, | I put my clothes under the bush, |
| 96 *tant que jeo revienc a maisun'.* | until that I return to home. | until I return home. |

| | Old French | Literal | English |
|---|---|---|---|
| 97 | La dame oï cele merveille, | The lady heard this marvel, | The lady heard this marvel, |
| 98 | de poür fu tute vermeille. | with fear became all crimson. | and became crimson with fear. |
| 99 | De l'aventure s'esfrea. | By the-event she-was-terrified. | By the event she was terrified. |
| 100 | En maint endreit se purpensa | In many ways she purposed | In many ways she thought, |
| 101 | cum ele s'en peüst partir; | how she if could part-with; | how she could part with him; |
| 102 | ne voleit mes lez lui gisir. | no-longer wanted with near him to-lie. | no longer did she want to lie near him. |
| 103 | Un chevalier de la cuntree, | A knight from the country, | A knight from the country, |
| 104 | ki lungement l'aveit amee | which long her-had loved | Who had long loved her |
| 105 | e mult preiee e mult requise | and much courted and much desired | and much courted and desired her |
| 106 | e mult duné en sun servise, | and much dedicated to her service, | and was much dedicated to her service, |
| 107 | (ele ne l'aveit unc amé | (she not him-had never loved | (she had never loved him, |
| 108 | ne de s'amur aseüré), | nor of love assured), | nor assured him of her love), |
| 109 | celui manda par sun message, | for-him sent-for by a message, | she sent for him by message, |
| 110 | si li descovri sun curage. | and to-him revealed her heart. | and revealed her sentiments to him. |
| 111 | Amis', fet ele, seiez liez! | 'Friend', said she, 'be happy! | Friend', she said, 'be happy! |
| 112 | Ceo dunt vus estes travailliez | That which you are striving | That what you have been striving for |
| 113 | vus otrei jeo senz nul respit; | you grant I without any delay; | I grant you without any delay; |
| 114 | ja n'i avrez nul cuntredit. | never none will have any opposition. | you will never have any opposition. |
| 115 | M'amur e mun cors vus otrei: | my-love and my body yours grant: | My love and my body I grant you: |

| | Old French | Literal | English |
|---|---|---|---|
| 116 | vostre drue faites de mei!' | your mistress make of me!' | make me your mistress!' |
| 117 | Cil l'en mercie bonement | This-he her thanks very-well | For this he thanks her very well |
| 118 | e la fiance de li prent, | and her promise of he receives, | and he receives her promise, |
| 119 | e el le met a sairement. | and she him puts under oath. | and she puts him under oath. |
| 120 | Puis li cunta cumfaitement | Then she recounted in-such-way | Then she told him which way |
| 121 | sis sire ala e qu'il devint. | her husband went and what became. | her husband went and what became of him. |
| 122 | Tute la veie que il tint | All the way that he travelled | The whole way that he travelled |
| 123 | vers la forest li enseigna; | to the forest she indicated; | to the forest she indicated; |
| 124 | pur sa despueille l'enveia. | for his clothes she-sent-for. | she sent him for her husband's clothes. |
| 125 | Issi fu Bisclavret traïz | Thus was Bisclavret betrayed | Thus was Bisclavret betrayed |
| 126 | e par sa femme mal bailliz. | and by this woman badly treated. | and treated badly by this woman. |
| 127 | Pur ceo qu'um le perdeit sovent, | Because that of-him one missed frequently, | Because he was frequently absent, |
| 128 | quidouent tuit comunalment | thought-they all together | they all thought together, |
| 129 | que dunc s'en fust del tut alez. | that so it was of all gone. | that he had gone for good. |
| 130 | Asez fu quis e demandez: | Much was he of sought-for: | Much was he sought and hunted for: |
| 131 | mes n'en porent mie trover, | but not could-they not-at-all find, | But they could not at all find him, |
| 132 | si lur estut laissier ester. | so let stand left was. | and so it was let be. |
| 133 | La dame a cil dunc espusee, | The woman then him so married, | The woman then married the one, |
| 134 | que lungement aveit amee. | who long had loved. | who had long lover her. |

| | Old French | Literal | English |
|---|---|---|---|
| 135 | *Issi remest un an entier,* | So remained one year entire, | So remained a whole year, |
| 136 | *tant que li reis ala chacier.* | until that the king of-the hunt. | until the king joined the hunt. |
| 137 | *A la forest ala tut dreit* | To the forest of all straight | to the forest his way led straight |
| 138 | *la u li Bisclavret esteit.* | there where he Bisclavret stayed. | there where the were Bisclavret stayed. |
| 139 | *Quant li chien furent descuplé,* | When the dogs were released, | When the dogs were released, |
| 140 | *le Bisclavret unt encuntré.* | the Bisclavret they encountered. | they encountered Bisclavret. |
| 141 | *A lui cururent tutejur* | Of him chased all-the-day | They chased him all day |
| 142 | *e li chien e li veneür,* | and the dogs and the hunters, | and the dogs and hunters, |
| 143 | *tant que pur poi ne l'ourent pris* | until which all but not caught prize | all but caught him |
| 144 | *e tut deciré e mal mis.* | and all tear and badly treated. | and all but tore and ripped him. |
| 145 | *Des que il a le rei choisi,* | Of when he of the king saw, | And when he saw the king, |
| 146 | *vers lui curut querre merci.* | went he running asking-for mercy. | He went running asking for mercy. |
| 147 | *Il l'aveit pris par sun estrié,* | He had seized by his stirrup, | He seized him by his stirrup, |
| 148 | *la jambe li baise e le pié.* | his leg he kisses and his feet. | kissed his legs and feet. |
| 149 | *Li reis le vit, grant poür a;* | The king him saw, great fear had; | When the king saw him, he had great fear; |
| 150 | *ses cumpaignuns tuz apela.* | his companions all he-called. | he called all his companions. |
| 151 | *Seignur', fet il, avant venez!* | 'Sires', said he, 'forward come! | 'Sires', he said, 'come forward! |
| 152 | *Iceste merveille esguardez,* | This marvel look-at, | Look at this marvel, |
| 153 | *cum ceste beste s'umilie!* | how this beast is-humbled! | how the beast is humbled! |

| | Old French | Literal | English |
|---|---|---|---|
| 154 | *Ele a sen d'ume, merci crie.* | He has sense of-a-man, mercy asks-for. | He has the sense of a man, who asks for mercy. |
| 155 | *Chaciez mei tuz cez chiens ariere,* | Chase from-me all these dogs back, | Chase from me all these dogs back, |
| 156 | *si guardez que hum ne la fiere!* | and take-care that he not is hit! | and take care that he is not hit!. |
| 157 | *Ceste beste a entente e sen.* | This beast has reason and sense. | This beast has reason and sense. |
| 158 | *Espleitiez vus! Alum nus en!* | Hurry you! Let-us we go! | Hurry! Let us all go! |
| 159 | *A la beste durrai ma pes:* | To the beast grant my peace: | To the beast grant my peace: |
| 160 | *kar jeo ne chacerai hui mes'.* | because I not will-hunt this-day furthermore. | Because from this day I do not wish to hunt any more. |
| 161 | *Li reis s'en est turnez a tant.* | The king then was returned at such-time. | The king then returned after a time. |
| 162 | *Li Bisclavret le vet siwant;* | The Bisclavret him there followed; | The Bisclavret followed him there; |
| 163 | *mult se tint pres, n'en volt partir,* | much he travels close, nor wants to-part, | he travels close to him, not wanting to leave him, |
| 164 | *il n'a cure de lui guerpir,* | he not-has care of him abandoning, | taking care not to abandon him, |
| 165 | *Li reis l'en meine en sun chastel.* | The king him takes to his castle. | The king takes him to his castle. |
| 166 | *Mult en fu liez, mult li est bel,* | Very he is happy, much he is well, | He is very happy, and very much well, |
| 167 | *kar unkes mes tel n'ot veü;* | because never he has before seen; | because he has never seen before; |
| 168 | *a grant merveille l'ot tenu* | a great wonder before beheld | a great wonder before beheld |
| 169 | *e mult le tint a grant chierté.* | and much him held of great fondness. | and he held him in great fondness. |
| 170 | *A tuz les suens a comandé* | Of all his people he commanded | Of all his people he commanded |
| 171 | *que sur s'amur le guardent bien* | for sure for-the-love-of him guard well | for the king's sake to guard him well |
| 172 | *e ne li mesfacent de rien,* | and not him harm of any, | and cause him no harm, |

| | Old French | Literal | English |
|---|---|---|---|
| 173 | ne par nul d'els ne seit feruz; | nor by anyone be he to-be beaten; | nor be beaten by anyone; |
| 174 | bien seit abevrez e peüz. | well to-be drink and food. | to be given drink and food. |
| 175 | Cil le guarderent volentiers | They him guarded gladly | They guarded him gladly. |
| 176 | tuz jurs entre les chevaliers, | all days among the knights, | All days he was among the knights, |
| 177 | e pres del rei s'alout culchier. | and close to the-king next-to slept. | And next to the king he slept. |
| 178 | N'i a celui ki ne l'ait chier; | No-one is who-him that not has love; | There is no one who does not love him; |
| 179 | tant esteit frans e de bon aire: | so noble engaging and of good appearance: | so noble engaging and of good appearance: |
| 180 | unkes ne volt a rien mesfaire. | never nor willed of anything misdeed. | never did he wish to do anything wrong. |
| 181 | U que li reis deüst errer, | Where which the king had to-go, | Where the king had to go, |
| 182 | il n'out cure de desevrer; | he not-had care of to-separate; | he did not care to separate from him; |
| 183 | ensemble od lui tuz jurs alout, | with among him all days he-went, | with him he always went, |
| 184 | bien s'aparceit que il l'amout. | well he-perceived that he him-loved. | and he perceived well that he loved him. |
| 185 | Oëz aprés cument avint! | Hear after what happened! | Hear what happened after! |
| 186 | A une curt que li reis tint | At a court which the king held | At a court which the king held |
| 187 | tuz les baruns aveit mandez, | all the barons he-had ordered, | he had ordered all the barons, |
| 188 | cels ki furent de ses chasez, | those which he-had of full fief, | those which he had fiefdom over, |
| 189 | pur aidier sa feste a tenir | for to-help his party to have | to contribute to his party |

| | Old French | Literal | English |
|---|---|---|---|
| 190 | e lui plus bel faire servir. | and him more well made served. | and serve him more graciously. |
| 191 | Li chevaliers i est alez, | The knight he is gone, | The knight he has gone, |
| 192 | richement e bien aturnez, | richly and well dressed, | richly and well dressed, |
| 193 | ki la femme Bisclavret ot. | who had the-wife Bisclavret of. | who had the wife of Bisclavret. |
| 194 | Il ne saveit ne ne quidot | He not knew not no thought | He did not know and did not think |
| 195 | qu'il le deüst trover si pres. | which-that he would find so close. | that he would find him so close. |
| 196 | Si tost cum il vint al palais | As soon as he came to the-palace | As soon as he came to the palace |
| 197 | e li Bisclavret l'aperceut, | and him Bisclavret noticed, | and Bisclavret noticed him, |
| 198 | de plein eslais vers lui curut: | of full run towards him ran: | at full speed he ran towards him: |
| 199 | as denz le prist, vers lui le trait. | in teeth his seized, towards him he draws. | in his teeth he seized him, toward him he draws him. |
| 200 | Ja li eüst mult grant laid fait, | Now he would-have much great harm done, | Now he would have done great harm, |
| 201 | ne fust li reis ki l'apela, | not had the king him called, | If the king had not called him, |
| 202 | d'une verge le manaça. | with-a stick him threatened. | and threatened him with a stick. |
| 203 | Dous feiz le volt mordre le jur. | Two times he wanted to-bite him that-day. | Twice that day he wanted to bite him. |
| 204 | Mult s'esmerveillent li plusur; | Most astonished him more; | Most people were more astonished; |
| 205 | kar unkes tel semblant ne fist | because never had appeared not been-so | because he had never appeared like this |
| 206 | vers nul hume que il veïst. | toward any man whom he saw. | toward any man whom he saw. |
| 207 | Ceo diënt tuit par la maisun | Everyone said all by the house | Everyone in the house said |
| 208 | qu'il nel fet mie senz raisun, | that not act not-at-all without reason, | that he did not act without a reason, |

| | Old French | Literal | English |
|---|---|---|---|
| 209 | mesfait li a, coment que seit, | mistreatment he had, somehow which been, | some injury or mistreatment had somehow been done to him, |
| 210 | kar volentiers se vengereit. | because he-wanted to avenge-himself. | because he wanted to avenge himself. |
| 211 | A cele feiz remest issi, | At that-time nothing more happened, | At that time nothing more happened, |
| 212 | tant que la feste departi; | until that the party departed; | until the party had departed; |
| 213 | e li barun unt pris cungié, | and the barons they took leave, | and the barons took leave, |
| 214 | a lur maisun sunt repairié. | to their homes they went. | and went to their homes. |
| 215 | Alez s'en est li chevaliers, | Gone it is the knight, | Gone is the knight, |
| 216 | mien esciënt tut as premiers, | among it-seems all the first, | among the first it seems, |
| 217 | que li Bisclavret asailli; | which the Bisclavret assailed; | which the Bisclavret had attacked; |
| 218 | n'est merveille s'il le haï. | not-is wonder if-him he hated. | no wonder if he hated him. |
| 219 | Ne fu puis guaires lungement, | Not happened since much long-after, | It happened not long after this, |
| 220 | (ceo m'est a vis, si cum j'entent), | (such is as so, if with I-understand), | (such as it is, if I understand), |
| 221 | qu'a la forest ala li reis, | that to-the forest went the king, | that the king went to the forest, |
| 222 | ki tant fu sages e curteis, | who was so understanding and courteous, | who was so understanding and courteous, |
| 223 | u li Bisclavret fu trovez; | where the Bisclavret was found; | to where the Bisclavret was found; |
| 224 | e il i est od lui alez. | and he with was among him went. | and there with him he went. |
| 225 | La nuit quant il s'en repaira, | The night when he was returned, | In the night when he came back, |
| 226 | en la cuntree herberja. | in the country he-stayed. | in the country he stayed. |
| 227 | La femme Bisclavret le sot. | The woman Bisclavret the found-out. | The wife of Bisclavret found out. |

| | Old French | Literal | English |
|---|---|---|---|
| 228 | Avenantment s'apareillot. | Attractively she-dressed. | Attractively she dressed. |
| 229 | Al demain vait al rei parler, | In the-morning went to-the king to-talk-with, | In the morning she went to see the king, |
| 230 | riche present li fait porter. | expensive present she does bring. | an expensive gift she brings him. |
| 231 | Quant Bisclavret la veit venir, | When Bisclavret her sees coming, | When Bisclavret sees her coming, |
| 232 | nuls huem nel poeit retenir: | none man not can retain-him: | no man can hold him back: |
| 233 | vers li curut cum enragiez. | towards her he-runs as-though enraged. | towards her he runs as though enraged. |
| 234 | Oëz cum il s'est bien vengiez! | Listen how he is well avenged! | Listen to how he is well avenged! |
| 235 | Le nes li esracha del vis. | Her nose he snatched from face. | Her nose he snatched from her face. |
| 236 | Que li peüst il faire pis? | What he worse he done could-have? | What worse could he have done? |
| 237 | De tutes parz l'unt manacié; | From all sides they threatened; | From all sides they threatened him; |
| 238 | ja l'eüssent tut depescié, | indeed they-would-have all dismembered, | indeed they would have dismembered him, |
| 239 | quant uns sages huem dist al rei: | when one wise man said to the-king: | when one wise man said to the king: |
| 240 | Sire', fet il, entent a mei! | 'Sire', said he, 'listen to me! | Sire', he said, 'listen to me!' |
| 241 | Ceste beste a esté od vus; | This beast has been with you; | This beast has been with you; |
| 242 | n'i a ore celui de nus | none is presently that-one of us | none of us who are present |
| 243 | ki ne l'ait veü lungement | who not has known-him long | have not known him long |
| 244 | e pres de lui alé sovent. | and close of him gone often. | and been close with him often. |
| 245 | Unkes mes hume ne tucha | Never more man not harm | Never more did he harm any man |
| 246 | ne felunie ne mustra, | nor felony none commit, | Nor commit any felony, |

| | Old French | Literal | English |
|---|---|---|---|
| 247 | *fors a la dame qu'ici vei.* | except to the woman who-here you-see. | except in the case of the woman you see here. |
| 248 | *Par cele fei que jeo vus dei,* | By that faith that I you owe, | By that faith I owe you, |
| 249 | *alkun curuz a il vers li* | some anger has he against her | he has some anger against her |
| 250 | *e vers sun seignur altresi.* | and against her husband also. | and against her husband also. |
| 251 | *Ceo est la femme al chevalier* | This is the wife of the-knight | This is the wife of the knight |
| 252 | *que tant suliëz aveir chier,* | whom that previously have loved, | whom you used to love, |
| 253 | *ki lung tens a esté perduz,* | who long held that was lost, | who for such a long time was lost, |
| 254 | *ne seümes qu'est devenuz.* | nor knew what became-of. | nor known what had become of him. |
| 255 | *Kar metez la dame en destreit,* | Therefore place the woman with difficulty, | Therefore force that woman's hand, |
| 256 | *s'alcune chose vus direit,* | if-some thing you tells, | so that she might tell you something, |
| 257 | *pur quei ceste beste la het.* | for what this beast her hates. | why this beast hates her. |
| 258 | *Faites li dire s'el le set!* | Makes her say if-she this knows! | Make her say if she knows why! |
| 259 | *Meinte merveille avum veüe* | Many wonders have-we seen | Many wonders we have seen |
| 260 | *ki en Bretaigne est avenue'.* | which in Brittany that happened. | which in Brittany that happened. |
| 261 | *Li reis a sun cunseil creü.* | The king of his counsel believed. | The king believed his counsel. |
| 262 | *Le chevalier a retenu;* | The knight was retained; | The knight was retained; |
| 263 | *de l'altre part la dame a prise* | of the-other part the woman was taken-aside | on the other hand, the woman was taken aside |
| 264 | *e en mult grant destresce mise.* | and then much great distress questioned. | and then distressed with many questions. |
| 265 | *Tant par destresce e par poür* | As-much by distress and by fear | As much by distress and by fear |

| | Old French | Literal | English |
|---|---|---|---|
| 266 | *tut li cunta de sun seignur,* | all she recounted of her husband, | she recounted all of her husband, |
| 267 | *coment ele l'aveit traï* | how she had betrayed | how she had betrayed him |
| 268 | *e sa despueille li toli,* | and how clothes his taken-away, | and how his clothes had been taken away, |
| 269 | *l'aventure qu'il li cunta,* | the-adventure which-of she recounted, | she told him of the adventure, |
| 270 | *e que devint e u ala;* | and what became and where he-went; | and what became of him and where he went; |
| 271 | *puis que ses dras li ot toluz,* | after that his clothes she away took, | after she took his clothes away, |
| 272 | *ne fu en sun païs veüz;* | not was he in country seen; | he was no longer seen in the country; |
| 273 | *tresbien quidot e bien creeit* | very-well thought that well believed | she thought and very well believed |
| 274 | *que la beste Bisclavret seit.* | that the beast Bisclavret to-be. | that the beast was Bisclavret. |
| 275 | *Li reis demande sa despueille.* | The king asked for the-clothing. | The king asks for the clothing. |
| 276 | *U bel li seit u pas nel vueille,* | Whether well he to-be or not nor want, | Whether he wants it or not, |
| 277 | *ariere la fet aporter,* | to-him it had brought, | to him it was brought, |
| 278 | *al Bisclavret la fist doner.* | to Bisclavret the has-it given. | to Bisclavret has it given. |
| 279 | *Quant il l'orent devant lui mise,* | When they had before him set, | When they put it before him, |
| 280 | *ne s'en prist guarde en nule guise.* | not did-he pay attention in no way. | he did not pay attention in any way. |
| 281 | *Li prozdum le rei apela,* | The worthy-man who the-king addressed, | The worthy man who addressed the king, |
| 282 | *cil ki primes le cunseilla.* | he who first him counselled. | he who first advised him. |
| 283 | *Sire, ne faites mie bien!* | 'Sire, not done not-at-all well! | Sire, it is not done well at all!' |
| 284 | *Cist nel fereit pur nule rien,* | The-last among doing by any nothing, | The last thing he will do, |
| 285 | *que devant vus ses dras reveste* | that before your sight clothes re-dress | is re-dress before your sight |
| 286 | *ne mut la semblance de beste.* | nor change his appearance from the-beast. | nor change his appearance from the beast. |

| | Old French | Literal | English |
|---|---|---|---|
| 287 | Ne savez mie que ceo munte. | You know not that this very-important. | You do not know that this is very important. |
| 288 | Mult durement en a grant hunte. | Very hard is a great shame. | Very hard is the great shame. |
| 289 | En tes chambres le fai mener | In your rooms him let be-taken | Let him be taken to your rooms, |
| 290 | e la despueille od lui porter; | and there clothes with him brought; | And have clothes brought to him; |
| 291 | une grant piece l'i laissuns. | a great part him let-us-leave. | And let us leave him for a time. |
| 292 | S'il devient huem, bien le verruns'. | if-he becomes a-man, well this we-will-see. | Whether he becomes a man, we will see. |
| 293 | Li reis meïsmes l'en mena | The king himself he there took | The king himself took him there |
| 294 | e tuz les hus sur lui ferma. | and all the doors behind him closed. | and all the doors behind him closed. |
| 295 | Al chief de piece i est alez; | At the-end of the-time there he went; | At the end of a time he went there; |
| 296 | dous baruns a od lui menez. | two barons that with him took. | he took two barons with him. |
| 297 | En la chambre entrerent tuit trei. | Unto the room entered all three. | All three entered the room. |
| 298 | Sur le demeine lit al rei | On his own bed the king's | On the king's own bed |
| 299 | truevent dormant le chevalier. | they-find sleeping the knight. | they find the knight sleeping. |
| 300 | Li reis le curut enbracier; | The king him ran to-embrace; | The king ran to embrace him; |
| 301 | plus de cent feiz l'acole e baise. | more than a-hundred times embraces and kisses. | more than a hundred times, he embraces and kisses him. |
| 302 | Si tost cum il pot aveir aise, | As soon as he could have facility, | As soon as he had the opportunity, |
| 303 | Tute sa terre li rendi, | All his land to-him returned, | He returned all his land to him, |
| 304 | plus li duna que jeo ne di. | more him gave than I can tell. | and gave him more than I can tell. |
| 305 | La femme a del païs ostee | The woman of from the-country banned | The woman was banned from the country |

|  | Old French | Literal | English |
|---|---|---|---|
| 306 | *e chaciee de la cuntree.* | and chased out-of the country. | and chased out of the country. |
| 307 | *Cil s'en ala ensemble od li,* | The-one who along together with her, | The one who went with her, |
| 308 | *pur qui sun seignur ot traï.* | for whom her husband had betrayed. | for whom she had betrayed her husband. |
| 309 | *Enfanz en a asez eüz,* | Children with of many they-had, | They had many children, |
| 310 | *puis unt esté bien cuneüz* | could they be well known | they were well known |
| 311 | *e del semblant e del visage:* | by of appearance and of face: | by their appearance and by their faces: |
| 312 | *plusurs des femmes del lignage,* | many of women of lineage, | many women of their lineage, |
| 313 | *c'est veritez, senz nes sunt nees* | it-is true, without noses they-were born | it is true, were born with out noses |
| 314 | *e si viveient esnasees.* | and thus they-live noselessly. | and so they lived noselessly. |
| 315 | *L'aventure qu'avez oïe* | The-story which you-heard | The story which you heard |
| 316 | *veraie fu, n'en dutez mie.* | true was, do-not doubt not-at-all. | was true, do not doubt at all. |
| 317 | *De Bisclavret fu fez li lais* | Of Bisclavret was composed this lay | This lay was composed of Bisclavret |
| 318 | *pur remembrance a tuz dis mais.* | for remembrance of all tell more. | for remembrance of all more to tell. |

# Word List *(Old French to English)*

| Old French | English | Old French | English |
|---|---|---|---|
| | | *ame* | somebody, soul |
| | | *amé* | loved |
| | | *amee* | loved |
| **A, a** | | *amer* | love |
| | | *amez* | a-love, loved |
| *a* | a, against, and, as, at, had, has, he, in, is, of, on, that, then, to, under, up to, was | *ami* | friend |
| | | *amie* | friend |
| | | *amis* | friend |
| | | *amistié* | friendship |
| *abatre* | destroy, knock down | *amor* | love |
| *abevrez* | drink | *amot* | loved |
| *acreanter* | agree, allow, promise | *an* | year |
| *ad* | against, in, on, to, up to | *anel* | ring |
| *adenz* | face downwards | *angregier* | become more painful, grow worse |
| *adober* | arm oneself | | |
| *adurer* | worship | *anima* | soul |
| *afaire* | matter | *anme* | somebody, soul |
| *ai* | have | *anor* | esteem, fief, honor, respect |
| *aidier* | to-help | | |
| *aiglantier* | wild rose | *anpur* | for the sake of |
| *aiglent* | wild rose | *aparant* | visible |
| *ainc* | earlier, rather | *aparceüz* | aware |
| *ains* | earlier, rather | *apela* | addressed, he-called |
| *ainz* | earlier, rather | *apeler* | accuse, call, summon |
| *aire* | appearance | *apercevoir* | know, notice |
| *aise* | facility | *apert* | manifest, open, visible |
| *aistre* | be | *aporter* | brought |
| *Al* | at, in, of, the, to, to-the | *apres* | after, afterwards |
| *ala* | along, he-went, of, of-the, went | *aprés* | after |
| | | *ardoir* | burn |
| *alaine* | blast, breath | *ardre* | burn |
| *alé* | gone | *argent* | money, riches, silver |
| *aleine* | blast, breath | *ariere* | back, to-him |
| *aler* | go | *arire* | back |
| *alez* | go, gone, went | *ariver* | arrive |
| *alkun* | some | *arme* | somebody, soul |
| *alme* | somebody, soul | *arrere* | back |
| *alne* | ell | *arriere* | back |
| *alout* | he-went, went | *art* | craft, liberal art |
| *alt* | high, important, strong | *as* | in, the |
| *altain* | deep, high | *asailli* | assailed |
| *altre* | other | *aseüré* | assured |
| *altresi* | also | *asez* | many, much, very well |
| *Alum* | let-us | | |
| *amant* | lover | | |

| Old French | English | Old French | English |
|---|---|---|---|
| asproier | prosecute, torment | baisier | kiss |
| assanler | assemble, call together, meet | balt | full of fervor, happy |
| assembler | assemble, call together, meet | barbe | beard |
| | | baron | brave knight, brave warrior |
| asseoir | lay siege, place, set up | barun | barons |
| assés | many, much, very well | baruns | barons |
| astenir | keep from | bataille | battle |
| ataindre | catch, reach, regain | Beals | handsome |
| atorner | prepare, turn | bealz | gentle |
| atot | with | bec | beak |
| aturnez | dressed | bel | beautiful, beloved, dear handsome, well |
| aucun | some | | |
| aussi | also, likewise | ben | good, good fortune, well-being |
| aut | high, important, strong | | |
| avant | forward | ber | baron |
| avec | with | beste | beast, the-beast |
| aveir | be, have | bevre | drink |
| aveit | had, he-had | bien | good, good fortune, many, much, really, well, well-being |
| avenant | attractive, beautiful | | |
| Avenantment | attractively | | |
| avenement | arrival | Bisclavret | werewolf |
| avenir | arrive, frequently, happen | blanc | white |
| | | blandi | cajoled |
| avenue | happened | bois | forest, tree |
| aviler | abandon, disgrace | bon | good |
| avint | happened | bonement | very-well |
| aviser | appreciate, look at, recognize, see | bons | good |
| | | bos | forest, tree |
| avoc | with | boscages | woods |
| avoir | be, have | bouche | mouth |
| avreie | could | braire | shout, sing |
| avrez | have | Bretaigne | Brittany |
| avuec | with | Bretan | Breton |
| avum | have-we | buche | mouth |
| | | buissun | bush |

# B, b

# C, c

| | | | |
|---|---|---|---|
| bacheler | page, young knight aspirant, young man | cadable | catapult |
| | | car | because, for |
| bachelor | page, young knight aspirant, young man | cas | affair, event, fall |
| | | castel | castle |
| baillier | give, own, receive | cavee | dug-out |
| bailliz | treated | ce | it, that, this |
| baisa | kissed | | |
| baise | kisses | | |

| Old French | English | Old French | English |
|---|---|---|---|
| *ceanz* | in here | *chiens* | dogs |
| *cel* | the | *chier* | love, loved |
| *cela* | concealed | *chierté* | fondness |
| *cele* | such, that, that-time, this | *choisi* | saw |
| | | *chose* | affair, creature, thing |
| *celer* | conceal | *chrestien* | christian |
| *cels* | those | *ci* | here |
| *celui* | for-him, that-one, who-him | *ciel* | heaven |
| | | *cil* | he, him, that, the-one, they, this-he |
| *cent* | a-hundred | | |
| *ceo* | behold-this, everyone, it, such, that, this | *Cist* | the-last, this |
| | | *cit* | city, town |
| *cervel* | brains | *citet* | city, town |
| *Cest* | this | *clameor* | appeal |
| *c'est* | it-is | *clamer* | call, confess, proclaim |
| *ceste* | this | *clementiam* | grace |
| *ceu* | it, that, this | *clerc* | clerk |
| *cez* | these | *clerge* | clerk |
| *chacerai* | will-hunt | *coer* | heart |
| *chaciee* | chased | *cointe* | clever, elegant, refined |
| *chacier* | hunt | *colomb* | dove, pigeon |
| *Chaciez* | chase | *colon* | dove, pigeon |
| *chaeir* | fall | *colpe* | mistake, sin |
| *chaitif* | miserable | *com* | as, in order that, when |
| *chaloir* | concern, matter | *comandé* | commanded |
| *chambre* | chamber, room, royal apartment, territory | *comander* | give, order, recommend |
| | | *comencier* | begin, start |
| *chambres* | rooms | *coment* | how, somehow |
| *chant* | melody, song | *comme* | as, when |
| *chanter* | sing | *compaigne* | troops |
| *chapele* | chapel | *comunalment* | together |
| *char* | flesh, meat | *concreidre* | give in |
| *charn* | flesh, meat | *congié* | leave, permission, permission to leave |
| *chartre* | agreement, letter | | |
| *chasez* | fief | *conquerre* | capture, conquer |
| *chasser* | hunt | *conseilleor* | advisor, counsellor |
| *chastel* | castle | *conseillier* | advisor, counsellor |
| *chemin* | path | *conserrer* | deprive, resign |
| *cheoir* | fall | *consirrer* | deprive, resign |
| *cher* | beloved, expensive | *consolation* | consolation |
| *chevalier* | knight, the-knight | *conte* | count |
| *chevaliers* | gentleman, knight, knights | *contenant* | appearance, demeanour, expression |
| *chevauchie* | expedition, ride | *conter* | count, relate |
| *chief* | head, the-end | *contre* | against, compared with |
| *chien* | dogs | *contredire* | oppose, resist |

| Old French | English |
|---|---|
| *converse* | about |
| *conversez* | about |
| *convoier* | escort |
| *cope* | mistake, sin |
| *cor* | heart, horn |
| *corn* | horn |
| *corocier* | afflict, anger |
| *corpe* | mistake, sin |
| *corre* | run |
| *cors* | body, heart |
| *cose* | affair, creature, thing |
| *couchier* | lie down |
| *creanter* | agree, grant |
| *creeit* | believed |
| *creistre* | grow |
| *creü* | believed |
| *crie* | asks-for |
| *criem* | fear |
| *crier* | shout |
| *croistre* | grow |
| *cruese* | hollow |
| *cuer* | heart, my-heart |
| *cuidier* | think |
| *cuire* | burn, cook |
| *culchier* | slept |
| *cum* | as, as-though, how, in order that, with |
| *cument* | what |
| *cumfaitement* | in-such-way |
| *cumpaignuns* | companions |
| *cuneüz* | known |
| *cunfort* | comfort |
| *cungié* | leave |
| *cunquerre* | capture, conquer |
| *cunseil* | counsel |
| *cunseilla* | counselled |
| *cunta* | recounted |
| *cunté* | recounted |
| *cunteneit* | led-himself |
| *cunter* | to-recount |
| *cuntredit* | opposition |
| *cuntree* | country |
| *curage* | heart |
| *cure* | anxiety, care |
| *curios* | careful |
| *curt* | court |

| Old French | English |
|---|---|
| *curteis* | courteous |
| *cururent* | chased |
| *curut* | anger, he-runs, ran, running |
| *curuz* | anger |

# D, d

| Old French | English |
|---|---|
| *daignier* | deign |
| *dales* | along, next to |
| *dallĂŠ* | along, next to |
| *dalles* | along, next to |
| *dam* | lord, sir |
| *damage* | harm, trouble |
| *dame* | dame, lady, madam, woman |
| *damoiselle* | girl of noble birth |
| *dan* | lord, sir |
| *de* | by, from, of, out-of, than, to, with |
| *de vers* | from the direction of, in the direction of |
| *deable* | devil |
| *debonaire* | noble, sweet |
| *deciré* | tear |
| *deçoivre* | deceive, mislead |
| *dedenz* | inside |
| *deduire* | lead, live |
| *degré* | staircase |
| *dei* | finger, owe |
| *del* | from, of, of-this, to |
| *delé* | next to; beside |
| *deleiz* | next to; beside |
| *deles* | next to; beside |
| *delicios* | delicious |
| *d'els* | be |
| *demain* | the-morning |
| *demanda* | questions |
| *demandasse* | to-ask |
| *demande* | asked |
| *demandé* | asked |
| *demander* | ask, ask for |
| *demandez* | ask, sought-for |
| *demeine* | own |
| *demoree* | delay, stay |

| Old French | English |
|---|---|
| demorer | remain, stay |
| demostrer | explaine, indicate, show |
| denz | teeth |
| departi | departed |
| depescié | dismembered |
| des | of, of-them |
| descendre | descend, dismount |
| desconfire | defeat, demolish |
| descovri | revealed |
| descuplé | released |
| desevrer | to-separate |
| desi | until |
| desos | under |
| desous | under |
| despueille | clothes, the-clothing |
| destreit | difficulty |
| destresce | distress |
| deu | god, god's |
| deüst | had, would |
| devant | before, in front of, in the presence of |
| deveneit | became |
| devenir | become |
| devenuz | became-of |
| devers | from the direction of, in the direction of |
| devez | should |
| deviene | become |
| devient | becomes |
| devindrent | became |
| devint | became |
| devoir | have to |
| devorer | devour |
| devure | devours |
| di | day, tell |
| diavle | devil |
| die | you |
| diënt | said |
| dirai | will-tell |
| dire | say, tell |
| direit | tells |
| dis | tell |
| dist | said, tell |
| dites | tell |
| divers | various |
| doi | finger |

| Old French | English |
|---|---|
| dol | grief, suffering |
| dolent | sorrowful, wetched |
| dolor | pain, suffering |
| dolur | pain |
| dolz | gentle, sweet |
| donc | then, therefore |
| doner | give, given |
| dont | of which, of whom, whose |
| dormant | sleeping |
| doter | be afraid, doubt |
| dous | gentle, sweet, two |
| dras | clothes |
| dreit | straight |
| droit | direct, proper, right |
| drue | mistress |
| duc | duke |
| duel | grief, suffering |
| dulz | sweet |
| d'ume | of-a-man |
| duna | gave |
| dunc | so |
| d'une | of-one, with-a |
| duné | dedicated |
| dunt | of which, of whom, which, whose |
| dur | cruel, hard, unrefined |
| durement | greatly, hard, sorely, very |
| durrai | grant |
| duter | doubt |
| dutez | doubt |

# E, e

| Old French | English |
|---|---|
| e | and, by, of, that |
| ed | and |
| eim | love |
| eissil | ruin, wretchedness |
| el | he, in, she |
| Ele | he, she |
| element | energy, force, god |
| emparenté | of noble lineage |
| empedement | persecution |
| empeindre | blow, protrude |

## Word List (Old French to English)

| Old French | English |
|---|---|
| empereor | emperor |
| en | and, go, he, in, into, is, of it, on, on top of, then, to, unto, with |
| enbracier | to-embrace |
| encombrer | overload |
| encontre | against, to, towards |
| encontrer | meet |
| encor | still, yet |
| encore | still, yet |
| encuntré | encountered |
| end | subsequently |
| endreit | immediately, precisely, right, ways |
| enemi | devil, enemy |
| Enfanz | children |
| enferm | crippled, ill, unhealthy, weak |
| enfermeté | illness, physical or moral weakness |
| enfern | hell |
| engagier | commit |
| engeignier | deceive, invent, seduce |
| engeindre | cause |
| engendrer | cause |
| engien | cheating, skill |
| engignier | deceive, invent, seduce |
| engin | cheating, skill |
| enne | not |
| ennui | grief |
| enoi | pain, torment |
| enor | esteem, fief, honor, respect |
| enorter | exhort, seduce, urge |
| enpur | for the sake of |
| enquis | inquired, queried |
| enragié | furious |
| enragiez | enraged |
| enseigna | indicated |
| enseigne | war cry |
| enseignier | inform, point out, teach |
| ensemble | together, with |
| ensemble od | together with |
| ent | subsequently |
| entendre | hear, pay attention, try, understand |
| entendu | heard |

| Old French | English |
|---|---|
| entent | listen |
| entente | reason |
| entier | entire |
| entiers | entire |
| entre | among, between, in the midst of |
| entrepris | unhappy person |
| entrerent | entered |
| enui | pain, torment |
| envers | towards |
| erbre | grass |
| errer | to-go |
| ert | was |
| es | in-those |
| esbai | frightened, surprised, troubled |
| esbanir | amuse |
| eschec | booty, loot |
| eschecs | chess |
| esciënt | it-seems |
| escïent | knowledge |
| escolter | listen to, pay attention to |
| escremir | fence |
| escrier | cry out, shout |
| escrimer | fence |
| escu | shield |
| esfrei | fear |
| esguardez | look-at |
| eslais | assault |
| esleecier | rejoice |
| esmaier | be dismayed |
| esnasees | noselessly |
| espee | sword |
| espés | thick |
| Espleitiez | hurry |
| esposer | marry |
| espuse | wife |
| espusee | married |
| esracha | snatched |
| essil | ruin, wretchedness |
| est | are, he, is, that, was |
| estait | standing |
| esté | be, been, was |
| esteit | he-was, noble, stayed, was-he |

| Old French | English | Old French | English |
|---|---|---|---|
| ester | be, remain, stand, was | fer | iron, weapon |
| estes | are | fereit | doing |
| estor | battle, noise, tumult | ferez | will-do |
| estorm | battle, noise, tumult | ferma | closed |
| estre | be, condition, life, way of life | feruz | beaten |
| estrié | stirrup | feste | party |
| estude | study, zeal | fet | act, had, said |
| estudie | study, zeal | feu | family, fire |
| estut | stand | fez | composed |
| et | and | fiance | promise |
| euc | this | fier | fierce, proud, strong |
| eure | hour, time | fiere | hit |
| eüsse | were | figure | character, form, person |
| eüst | would-have | fil | son |
| eüz | they-had | filer | spin |
| | | fille | daughter |
| | | filuel | godson, son |
| | | finir | end, stop |

## F, f

| Old French | English | Old French | English |
|---|---|---|---|
| | | fist | been-so, has-it |
| | | flor | flower |
| fai | let | florir | flower |
| faim | desire, hunger | foi | faith, honor |
| faire | do, done, made, make | fol | crazy |
| faiseit | made | foler | harm |
| fait | does, done, has-done, said | forest | forest |
| faites | done, make, makes | forez | forests |
| faldestoed | folding chair for important person, throne | forfait | committed |
| | | forment | greatly, very, very much |
| faldestuef | folding chair for important person, throne | fors | except, out, outside |
| | | fort | fierce, hard, strong |
| | | fou | family, fire |
| faldestuel | folding chair for important person, throne | fraindre | break |
| | | frans | engaging |
| | | freindre | break |
| fals | false | frere | brother |
| faus | false | fromage | cheese |
| favele | lie, story | fu | became, happened, is, so, was |
| fei | faith, honor | fuier | abandon, flee from |
| feindre | do nothing, shy away | fuir | abandon, flee from |
| feintise | deceit, pretense | furent | he-had, were |
| feiz | nothing, put, time, times | fusse | had-been |
| felunie | felony | fussent | would-be |
| femme | the-wife, wife, woman | fust | had, was |
| femmes | women | | |
| fenir | end, stop | | |

| Old French | English | Old French | English |
|---|---|---|---|
| | | *halberc* | hauberk |
| | | *halt* | high, important, strong |
| **G, g** | | *hardi* | bold, brave |
| | | *hastif* | swift |
| *gab* | jest | *have* | dark, sick, somber |
| *gant* | glove | *herbergier* | lodge, receive as guest shelter |
| *garant* | defense, protection | | |
| *garder* | guard, watch over | *herberja* | he-stayed |
| *garent* | defense, protection | *het* | hates |
| *garnement* | decorative object | *home* | man |
| *Garulf* | Garulf | *honestét* | honor |
| *gent* | beautiful, fair, handsome, people, race | *honore* | honored |
| | | *honte* | disgrace, shame |
| *gentil* | brave, noble | *hors* | except, out, out of |
| *gesir* | lie | *huem* | a-man, man |
| *geter* | reject, throw, utter | *hui* | this-day |
| *gisir* | to-lie | *huit* | eight |
| *giter* | reject, throw, utter | *huitaves* | octave |
| *gloire* | glory | *hum* | he, him |
| *grabatum* | simple bed | *hume* | man |
| *grant* | great, large, tall | *humes* | men |
| *granter* | agree, grant | *hunte* | shame |
| *granz* | grand | *hus* | doors |
| *gré* | Greek | | |
| *gri* | Greek | | |
| *grieu* | Greek | **I, i** | |
| *griu* | Greek | | |
| *guaires* | much | | |
| *gualdine* | forest | *i* | he, i, is, there, with |
| *guarde* | attention | *Iceste* | this |
| *guardent* | guard | *ici* | here |
| *guarderent* | guarded | *iestre* | be |
| *guardez* | take-care | *Il* | he, it, they |
| *guarie* | relieved | *ilec* | there |
| *guerpir* | abandon, abandoning, leave | *ille* | island |
| | | *iluec* | there |
| *guerre* | trouble, war | *iluoc* | there |
| *guerredoner* | reward | *ire* | anger, distress |
| *guise* | manner, way | *iré* | angry, distressed, furious |
| *gunfanuner* | standard bearer | | |
| | | *irié* | angry, distressed, furious |
| **H, h** | | *isle* | island |
| | | *issi* | happened, here, so, thus |
| *ha* | ha, hello | | |
| *haï* | hated | *issil* | ruin, wretchedness |
| *haine* | hatred | *issir* | come out, go out |

| Old French | English | Old French | English |
|---|---|---|---|
| | | laissuns | let-us-leave |
| | | l'ait | has |
| | | l'altre | the-other |
| **J, j** | | l'amout | him-loved |
| | | l'anguissa | anguish |
| ja | already, at once, ever, indeed, never, now | l'apela | called |
| Jadis | days-passed | l'apelent | they-call |
| jai | already, at once, now | l'aperceut | noticed |
| jambe | leg | l'aveit | had, her-had, him-had |
| j'entent | i-understand | l'aventure | the-adventure, the-event, the-story |
| jeo | I | le | he, her, him, his, it, one, the, this, who |
| jes | I | | |
| jeu | I | leal | legitimate, loyal |
| jo | I, me | lee | wide |
| joer | play | legier | light, light-hearted, supple |
| joi | joy | | |
| joie | joy | l'en | her, him, there |
| joieus | full of joy | l'enveia | she-sent-for |
| joius | joyous | les | his, let, the |
| jol | I | leur | their |
| jor | day | l'eüssent | they-would-have |
| jorn | day | lever | lift up |
| jornee | day's journey | lez | near |
| jou | I | li | he, her, him, his, she, the, this, to-him, was |
| jur | that-day | | |
| jurs | days | l'i | him |
| jusqu'a | as far as, up to | lié | happy, joyful |
| | | lier | bind |
| **K, k** | | liet | happy, joyful |
| | | liez | happy |
| kar | because, come, therefore | ligier | light, light-hearted, supple |
| ki | him, of, that, which, who | lignage | family, lineage |
| | | lil | lily |
| **L, l** | | lit | bed |
| | | liue | mile |
| la | had, her, his, is, it, of, that, the, there, to-the | live | mile |
| | | livre | book, inventory |
| l'a | that, this | loër | praise |
| l'acola | he-embraced | l'oï | that-heard |
| l'acole | embraces | loial | legitimate, loyal |
| l'ai | of-him | loier | bind |
| laid | harm | loigier | light, light-hearted, supple |
| lais | lay, lays | loin | far, far away |
| laissier | abandon, leave, left, let | loing | far, far away, long |

| Old French | English | Old French | English |
|---|---|---|---|
| *lonc* | far, far away, long | *manjuer* | eat |
| *long* | far, long | *mar* | in vain, wrongly |
| *longement* | for a long time, long | *masse* | mass |
| *lor* | their | *mat* | exhausted, feeble, sad |
| *l'orent* | had | *me* | I, me, to-me |
| *losenja* | praised | *mectre* | put |
| *l'ot* | before | *mei* | from-me, me, mine, to-me |
| *l'ourent* | caught | | |
| *lui* | he, him | *meine* | takes |
| *luin* | far, far away | *meins* | fewer, less |
| *lung* | long | *meinte* | many |
| *lungement* | long, long-after | *meïsmes* | himself, myself |
| *l'unt* | they | *mels* | better, rather |
| *lur* | let, their | *m'en* | to-me |
| | | *mena* | took |
| | | *menace* | menace |
| | | *mener* | be-taken, lead, show, take |

# M, m

| Old French | English | Old French | English |
|---|---|---|---|
| *ma* | my | *menestier* | profession, service |
| *magne* | great | *menez* | took |
| *maindre* | remain, stay | *mentir* | betray, deny, fail, lie |
| *mains* | fewer, less | *m'entremet* | i-begin |
| *maint* | many, many a | *menu* | quickly |
| *maintenant* | immediately, soon | *menut* | quickly |
| *mais* | but, further, more, rather | *mer* | pure, sea |
| | | *merci* | grace, mercy, pity |
| *maisnie* | army, household | *mercie* | thanks |
| *maisniee* | army, household | *mere* | mother |
| *maison* | house | *merveille* | marvel, marvellously, what is surprising, wonder, wonders |
| *maisun* | home, homes, house | | |
| *mal* | bad, badly, disaster, evil, harm, illness, mean, wretched | *mes* | but, furthermore, he, me, more, my, with |
| *malement* | badly | *mescroire* | refuse to believe, suspect |
| *malfé* | demon, devil | | |
| *Mals* | bad | *meserrez* | misguided |
| *maltalent* | anger | *mesfacent* | harm |
| *m'amur* | my-love | *mesfaire* | misdeed |
| *manaça* | threatened | *mesfait* | mistreatment |
| *manace* | menace | *mesprendre* | commit a crime, make a mistake |
| *manacié* | threatened | | |
| *manda* | sent-for | *message* | message, messenger |
| *mandez* | ordered | *m'est* | is |
| *maneit* | lived | *met* | go, put, puts |
| *mangier* | eat | *metez* | place |
| *maniere* | intention, way | *metre* | put |
| | | *mettre* | put |

*Word List (Old French to English)*

| Old French | English |
|---|---|
| mie | not, not-at-all |
| miels | better, rather |
| mien | among |
| mier | pure |
| millier | thousand |
| miracle | miracle |
| mis | treated |
| mise | questioned, set |
| moine | monk |
| moins | fewer, less |
| molt | many, much, very |
| mon | my |
| monie | monk |
| mont | mountain |
| montaigne | mountain |
| moralité | character, lesson |
| mordre | to-bite |
| morir | die, kill |
| mort | death |
| mot | word |
| mout | many, much, very |
| mult | many, most, much, very |
| mun | my, to-me |
| mund | world |
| munte | very-important |
| mur | wall |
| mustra | commit |
| mut | change |

# N, n

| Old French | English |
|---|---|
| n'a | not-has |
| nate | matting |
| ne | and not, can, he, naught, no, no-longer, none, nor, not, you |
| nees | born |
| nef | ship |
| nel | among, nor, not |
| nen | do-not, not |
| n'en | about, do-not, nor, not |
| nes | nose, noses |
| n'est | not-is |
| neveu | grandson, nephew |
| nevot | grandson, nephew |

| Old French | English |
|---|---|
| ni | and not, nor |
| n'i | never-will, none, No-one |
| niënt | nothing |
| nïent | not at all |
| noblement | nobly |
| nom | name, title |
| nomer | call, name |
| non | name, not, title |
| noncier | announce, tell |
| nonque | never |
| nonsavoir | ignorance |
| Norman | Normans |
| nos | we |
| nostre | our |
| n'ot | before |
| n'out | not-had |
| nuit | night |
| nul | any, anyone, no, not any |
| nule | any, no, not |
| nuls | none |
| nun | the-name |
| nus | us, we |
| nuz | nude |

# O, o

| Old French | English |
|---|---|
| o | or, this, with |
| ocire | kill |
| od | among, with |
| odir | hear |
| oeuil | eye |
| Oëz | hear, listen |
| of | with |
| oi | today |
| oï | heard, i-hear |
| oïe | you-heard |
| oil | eye |
| oir | hear |
| oïr | hear |
| oisel | bird |
| olifant | ivory horn |
| om | one |
| ome | man |

| Old French | English | Old French | English |
|---|---|---|---|
| on | one | parole | speech, word |
| onor | esteem, fief, honor, respect | part | part, portion |
| | | partez | part |
| onques | ever, once | partir | part-with, to-part |
| or | gold, just, now | partirai | will-part |
| oraison | prayer, speech | parvenir | arrive |
| ore | hour, now, presently, time | parz | sides |
| | | pas | not |
| orer | pray | pau | few, little |
| orison | prayer, speech | pechié | mistake, sin |
| osasse | dare | pecier | smash to pieces |
| osberc | hauberk | peine | suffering, torment |
| oser | dare | pendre | hang |
| ostee | banned | pener | suffer, torture |
| ostel | dwelling, house | penser | pay attention, think |
| ot | away, had, of, with | peor | fear |
| otrei | grant | perdeit | lost, missed |
| otrier | agree, grant | perdrai | destroy |
| otroier | agree, grant | perdre | lose, loss, perish |
| ou | this, where | perduz | lost, to-lose |
| | | pere | father |

## P, p

| Old French | English | Old French | English |
|---|---|---|---|
| | | peril | danger |
| | | perir | destroy, perish |
| pagien | heathen, pagan | perte | destruction, fall |
| paien | heathen, pagan | pes | peace |
| paile | precious cloth | pestre | feed |
| pain | bread | petit | little, small |
| paine | suffering, torment | peüst | could, worse |
| païs | country, the-country | peüz | food |
| paistre | feed | pié | feet, foot |
| palais | the-palace | piece | part, piece, segment, the-time |
| pance | belly, stomach | | |
| paor | fear | piere | prison, stone |
| Par | by, by reason of, through | pierre | prison, stone |
| | | pin | pine tree |
| par mi | in the middle, through | pis? | could-have |
| parage | family, origin, rank | plain | full |
| parament | finery, precious object | plaindre | complain, mourn, regret |
| pardon | grace, permission | plaire | please |
| pardoner | forgive, pardon | plein | full |
| parent | father, parent | ploier | bend, yield |
| parlement | conversation, meeting, word | plorer | cry, shed tears |
| | | pluisor | several |
| parler | speak, talk, to-talk-with | plus | more, most |
| parmi | in the middle, through | plusor | several |
| | | plusur | many, more |

| Old French | English | Old French | English |
|---|---|---|---|
| plusurs | many | pui | hill, mountain |
| poeir | be able, can | puis | after, could, since, subsequently, then |
| poeit | can, could | pur | all, because, by, for, therefore |
| poi | but, few, little | | |
| poier | be able, can | purpensa | purposed |
| polle | girl | | |
| pooir | be able, can | | |
| por | for | **Q, q** | |
| porchacier | pursue, seek | | |
| porent | could-they | qu'a | that |
| porofrir | present | Qu'ai | what-have |
| port | harbour, port | quanque | all that |
| porter | bring, brought, carry, wear | Quant | when |
| | | quar | because, for |
| porveor | purveyor | qu'avez | which |
| post | after | que | for, than, that, what, when, which, who |
| pot | could | | |
| pou | few, little | quei | what |
| poür | fear, horror | quel | what, which |
| pout | could | qu'el | with |
| poverté | misery, poverty | queloigne | distaff |
| povre | poor | qu'en | that-in |
| preie | plunder | quenoille | distaff |
| preiee | courted | quere | ask, look for, want |
| preier | beg, beseech, pray | querre | ask, asking-for, look for, want |
| premiers | first | | |
| prendre | seize, take, take hold of | querrez | ask |
| prent | receives | qu'est | what |
| pres | close | qui | that, what, who |
| pres de | close to | qu'ici | who-here |
| present | present | quidot | thought |
| presenter | bring before the judge, offer, present | quidouent | thought-they |
| | | qu'il | that, what, which, which-of, which-that |
| prester | lend | | |
| priement | prayer | quinze | fifteen |
| prier | beg, beseech, pray | quis | he |
| primes | first | qu'um | of-him |
| pris | prize, seized, took | | |
| prise | taken-aside | **R, r** | |
| prisier | appreciate, esteem | | |
| prison | captivity, prison | rage | rage |
| prist | pay, seized | raine | queen |
| privez | close | raison | reason, speech, word |
| proisier | appreciate, esteem | raisun | reason |
| prozdum | worthy-man | ravine | theft |
| pucele | girl, maiden, servant | | |

33

| Old French | English | Old French | English |
|---|---|---|---|
| ravoir | have back | riche | expensive, generous, powerful, strong |
| ré | stake | | |
| reclamer | beg, call upon, invoke | richement | richly |
| reconoistre | recognize | rien | any, anything, creature, nothing, person, thing |
| recreant | cowardly, exhausted | | |
| redoter | be afraid, fear | rien? | nothing |
| redut | dread | roi | king |
| refaire | repair | roine | queen |
| regal | of the king, royal | rompre | break, burst |
| regem | king | rose | rose |
| regne | country, kingdom | rover | ask, call upon, order |
| rei | king, king's, stake, the-king | rue | street, village |
| reine | queen | | |
| reis | king | | |

# S, s

| Old French | English | Old French | English |
|---|---|---|---|
| relef | remains, scraps | sa | for, his, how, this |
| remanoir | remain, resist, stay | sages | understanding, wise |
| remembrance | rememberance | sai | i-know |
| remest | more, remained | saige | clever, educated |
| ren | creature, person, thing | saint | holy |
| rendi | returned | sairement | oath |
| rendre | give, return | saive | clever, educated |
| rendu | returned | s'alcune | if-some |
| renier | abjure, deny | s'alout | next-to |
| renoier | abjure, deny | saluer | greet, salute |
| repaira | returned | salvage | savage |
| repairié | went | s'amur | for-the-love-of, love |
| repairiez | returned | sanc | blood |
| requerre | ask, beseech | sanglent | bloody |
| requise | desired | santé | health, well-being |
| resort | defense, remedy, restriction | s'aparceit | he-perceived |
| resovenir | remember | s'apareillot | she-dressed |
| respit | delay | saveit | knew, knowing |
| respondre | answer | s'aventure | his-adventure |
| respunt | responded | savez | know |
| retenir | retain-him | savoir | know |
| retenu | retained | se | he, if, of, she, to |
| retor | return | se coucher | lie down |
| retorn | return | se dementer | lament |
| reveler | make known, reveal, revolt | se departir | go away, leave |
| reveste | re-dress | se faire | be |
| revienc | return | se hasteier | hasten |
| rez | stake | se haster | hasten |
| | | se pasmer | faint, swoon |
| | | se reposer | rest |

34

| Old French | English |
|---|---|
| seans | in here |
| secle | earthly life, world |
| secorer | go to the help of |
| seiez | be |
| seignor | lord |
| seignur | husband, lord, sires |
| seit | been, to-be |
| s'el | if-she |
| semblance | appearance |
| semblant | appearance, appeared |
| semblereit | would-look-like |
| semeine | week |
| sempre | always, immediately |
| sempres | always, immediately |
| sen | direction, sense |
| s'en | did-he, if, it, then, was, who |
| sens | direction, sense |
| sentier | path |
| sentir | feel, smell |
| senz | without |
| seoir | be seated, sit |
| sereie | I-would-be |
| serre | prison |
| servant | servant |
| servir | serve, served |
| servise | devotion, favor, service, task |
| ses | full, his, sight |
| s'esfrea | she-was-terrified |
| s'esmerveillent | astonished |
| s'est | is |
| set | knows, seven |
| seü | known |
| seule | earthly life, world |
| seümes | knew |
| seur | above, on, over, sure, to |
| si | and, and moreover, and thus, as, but, if, so, that much, that way, thus, yet |
| s'i | thus |
| siecle | earthly life, world |
| S'il | if-he, if-him, whether |
| sire | husband, my-lord, sire |
| sis | her |

| Old French | English |
|---|---|
| siwant | followed |
| soens | his |
| sol | alone |
| soloir | be accustomed |
| som | sleep |
| some | sleep |
| son | his |
| soner | sound, utter |
| sor | above, on, over, to |
| sos | under |
| sostenir | support, sustain |
| sot | found-out |
| soure | above, on, over, to |
| sout | knew |
| sovent | frequently, many, often, time-to-time |
| soz | under |
| sucurs | help |
| suens | people |
| sui | am, i-am |
| suleit | used |
| suliëz | previously |
| s'umilie | is-humbled |
| sun | a, her, his, in |
| suner | sound, utter |
| sunt | are, they, they-were |
| sur | above, behind, on, over, sure, to |
| sus | above, up |
| Suventes | repeatedly |
| suz | above, under, up |
| suzprist | under-pressed |

# T, t

| Old French | English |
|---|---|
| table | game, table |
| tans | time, weather |
| tant | as, as-much, so, so much, so-much, such, such-time, that, until |
| tantost | immediately |
| tel | had, has, much, such |
| temple | forehead, temple |
| tendrement | tenderly |

| Old French | English | Old French | English |
|---|---|---|---|
| *tenir* | consider, have, hold, keep, seize | *trovez* | found |
| *tens* | held, time, weather | *truevent* | they-find |
| *tenu* | beheld | *trusqu'* | until, up to |
| *terme* | period, period of time, term | *tu* | you |
| | | *tucha* | harm |
| *termine* | period of time | *tuit* | all |
| *terre* | country, earth, land | *turnez* | returned |
| *tes* | your | *tut* | all |
| *teste* | head | *tute* | all |
| *tindrent* | had | *tutejur* | all-the-day |
| *tint* | held, travelled, travels | *tutes* | all |
| *tirer* | pull | *tuz* | all, totally |
| *toli* | taken-away | | |
| *tolir* | cut off, take off | | |
| *toluz* | took | | |

## U, u

| Old French | English |
|---|---|
| *ton* | your |
| *tor* | tower |
| *torner* | return, turn |
| *tornoier* | tourney, whirl around |
| *tort* | mistake |
| *tost* | immediately, quickly, soon |
| *tot* | all, completely, entirely, every, whole |

| *u* | or, where, whether |
|---|---|
| *ubliër* | forget |
| *ue* | today |
| *ui* | today |
| *un* | a, one |
| *unc* | never |
| *uncore* | still, yet |
| *une* | a, an, one |
| *unkes* | never |
| *uns* | one |
| *unt* | then, they |

| *traï* | betrayed |
|---|---|
| *trair* | betray |
| *traist* | drew-close |
| *trait* | draws |
| *traïz* | betrayed |
| *travailliez* | striving |
| *trei* | three |

## V, v

| *treis* | three |
|---|---|
| *trembler* | tremble |
| *trenchier* | cut |
| *trente et quatre* | thirty four |
| *tres* | much, very |
| *tresbien* | very-well |
| *trespasser* | cross, go by, pass |
| *tresprendre* | overcome completely |
| *tresqu'* | until, up to |
| *tristece* | horror, sadness |
| *trois* | three |
| *trop* | excessively, extremely, too much |
| *trover* | find |

| *vaillant* | valiant |
|---|---|
| *vain* | empty, weak |
| *vait* | goes, went |
| *veer* | forbid, refuse |
| *vei* | you-see |
| *veie* | road, way |
| *veil* | old |
| *veintre* | conquer, overcome, vanquish |
| *veisins* | neighbours |
| *veïst* | saw |
| *veit* | sees |
| *veiz* | time |
| *vendra* | comes |
| *veneür* | hunters |

*Word List (Old French to English)*

| Old French | English |
|---|---|
| *venez* | come |
| *vengereit* | avenge-himself |
| *vengiez* | avenged |
| *venir* | come, coming, go |
| *venue* | arrival |
| *veoir* | see |
| *verai* | real, true |
| *veraie* | true |
| *verge* | stick |
| *vergier* | garden, orchard |
| *veritez* | true |
| *vermeille* | crimson |
| *verruns* | we-will-see |
| *vers* | against, to, toward, towards, went |
| *vert* | green |
| *vertu* | might, power, strength |
| *vestuz* | dressed |
| *vet* | goes, there |
| *veü* | known-him, seen |
| *vieil* | old |
| *viez* | old |
| *vif* | live |
| *vilain* | bad, ugly |
| *vin* | wine |
| *vint* | came |
| *virge* | virgin |
| *virginitét* | christian purity, spiritual purity |
| *vis* | face, so |
| *visage* | face |
| *viseter* | observe, visit |
| *vit* | saw |
| *viveient* | they-live |
| *voir* | indeed, true, truly |
| *voirement* | really |
| *vois* | go, noise, voice, word |
| *voiz* | noise, voice, word |
| *voleit* | wanted |
| *volentiers* | gladly, he-wanted, willing |
| *voler* | fly |
| *voloir* | want |
| *volt* | wanted, wants, willed |
| *vos* | you |
| *vostre* | your |

| Old French | English |
|---|---|
| *voz* | your |
| *vueil* | i-want, i-wish, want |
| *vueille* | want |
| *vuide* | empty |
| *vuit* | empty |
| *vus* | answer, i-wish, you, you-have, your, yours |

# Word List *(English to Old French)*

| English | Old French | English | Old French |
|---------|-----------|---------|-----------|
| | | and moreover | *si* |
| | | and not | *ne, ni* |
| | | and thus | *si* |

## A, a

| English | Old French |
|---------|-----------|
| a | *a, sun, un, une* |
| abandon | *aviler, fuier, fuir, guerpir, laissier* |
| abandoning | *guerpir* |
| abjure | *renier, renoier* |
| about | *converse, conversez, n'en* |
| above | *seur, sor, soure, sur, sus, suz* |
| accuse | *apeler* |
| act | *fet* |
| addressed | *apela* |
| advisor | *conseilleor, conseillier* |
| affair | *cas, chose, cose* |
| afflict | *corocier* |
| after | *apres, aprés, post, puis* |
| afterwards | *apres* |
| against | *a, ad, contre, encontre, vers* |
| agree | *acreanter, creanter, granter, otrier, otroier* |
| agreement | *chartre* |
| a-hundred | *cent* |
| all | *pur, tot, tuit, tut, tute, tutes, tuz* |
| all that | *quanque* |
| allow | *acreanter* |
| all-the-day | *tutejur* |
| alone | *sol* |
| along | *ala, dales, dallĂŠ, dalles* |
| a-love | *amez* |
| already | *ja, jai* |
| also | *altresi, aussi* |
| always | *sempre, sempres* |
| am | *sui* |
| a-man | *huem* |
| among | *entre, mien, nel, od* |
| amuse | *esbanir* |
| an | *une* |
| and | *a, e, ed, en, et, si* |

| English | Old French |
|---------|-----------|
| and moreover | *si* |
| and not | *ne, ni* |
| and thus | *si* |
| anger | *corocier, curut, curuz, ire, maltalent* |
| angry | *iré, irié* |
| anguish | *l'anguissa* |
| announce | *noncier* |
| answer | *respondre, vus* |
| anxiety | *cure* |
| any | *nul, nule, rien* |
| anyone | *nul* |
| anything | *rien* |
| appeal | *clameor* |
| appearance | *aire, contenant, semblance, semblant* |
| appeared | *semblant* |
| appreciate | *aviser, prisier, proisier* |
| are | *est, estes, sunt* |
| arm oneself | *adober* |
| army | *maisnie, maisniee* |
| arrival | *avenement, venue* |
| arrive | *ariver, avenir, parvenir* |
| as | *a, com, comme, cum, Si, tant* |
| as far as | *jusqu'a* |
| ask | *demander, demandez, quere, querre, querrez, requerre, rover* |
| ask for | *demander* |
| asked | *demande, demandé* |
| asking-for | *querre* |
| asks-for | *crie* |
| as-much | *tant* |
| assailed | *asailli* |
| assault | *eslais* |
| assemble | *assanler, assembler* |
| assured | *aseüré* |
| as-though | *cum* |
| astonished | *s'esmerveillent* |
| at | *a, Al* |
| at once | *ja, jai* |
| attention | *guarde* |
| attractive | *avenant* |

| English | Old French |
|---|---|
| attractively | *Avenantment* |
| avenged | *vengiez* |
| avenge-himself | *vengereit* |
| aware | *aparceüz* |
| away | *ot* |

# B, b

| English | Old French |
|---|---|
| back | *ariere, arire, arrere, arriere* |
| bad | *mal, Mals, vilain* |
| badly | *mal, malement* |
| banned | *ostee* |
| baron | *ber* |
| barons | *barun, baruns* |
| battle | *bataille, estor, estorm* |
| be | *aistre, aveir, avoir, d'els, esté, ester, estre, iestre, se faire, seiez* |
| be able | *poeir, poier, pooir* |
| be accustomed | *soloir* |
| be afraid | *doter, redoter* |
| be dismayed | *esmaier* |
| be seated | *seoir* |
| beak | *bec* |
| beard | *barbe* |
| beast | *beste* |
| beaten | *feruz* |
| beautiful | *avenant, bel, gent* |
| became | *deveneit, devindrent, devint, fu* |
| became-of | *devenuz* |
| because | *car, kar, Pur, quar* |
| become | *devenir, deviene* |
| become more painful | *angregier* |
| becomes | *devient* |
| bed | *lit* |
| been | *esté, seit* |
| been-so | *fist* |
| before | *devant, l'ot, n'ot* |
| beg | *preier, prier, reclamer* |
| begin | *comencier* |
| beheld | *tenu* |
| behind | *sur* |
| behold-this | *ceo* |

| English | Old French |
|---|---|
| believed | *creeit, creü* |
| belly | *pance* |
| beloved | *bel, cher* |
| bend | *ploier* |
| beseech | *preier, prier, requerre* |
| be-taken | *mener* |
| betray | *mentir, trair* |
| betrayed | *traï, traïz* |
| better | *mels, miels* |
| between | *entre* |
| bind | *lier, loier* |
| bird | *oisel* |
| Bisclavret | *Bisclavret* |
| blast | *alaine, aleine* |
| blood | *sanc* |
| bloody | *sanglent* |
| blow | *empeindre* |
| body | *cors* |
| bold | *hardi* |
| book | *livre* |
| booty | *eschec* |
| born | *nees* |
| brains | *cervel* |
| brave | *gentil, hardi* |
| brave knight | *baron* |
| brave warrior | *baron* |
| bread | *pain* |
| break | *fraindre, freindre, rompre* |
| breath | *alaine, aleine* |
| Breton | *Bretan* |
| bring | *porter* |
| bring before the judge | *presenter* |
| Brittany | *Bretaigne* |
| brother | *frere* |
| brought | *aporter, porter* |
| burn | *ardoir, ardre, cuire* |
| burst | *rompre* |
| bush | *buissun* |
| but | *mais, mes, poi, si* |
| by | *de, e, Par, pur* |
| by reason of | *par* |

# C, c

| English | Old French |
|---|---|
| cajoled | *blandi* |
| call | *apeler, clamer, nomer* |
| call together | *assanler, assembler* |
| call upon | *reclamer, rover* |
| called | *l'apela* |
| came | *vint* |
| can | *ne, poeir, poeit, poier, pooir* |
| captivity | *prison* |
| capture | *conquerre, cunquerre* |
| care | *cure* |
| careful | *curios* |
| carry | *porter* |
| castle | *castel, chastel* |
| catapult | *cadable* |
| catch | *ataindre* |
| caught | *l'ourent* |
| cause | *engeindre, engendrer* |
| chamber | *chambre* |
| change | *mut* |
| chapel | *chapele* |
| character | *figure, moralité* |
| chase | *Chaciez* |
| chased | *chaciee, cururent* |
| cheating | *engien, engin* |
| cheese | *fromage* |
| chess | *eschecs* |
| children | *Enfanz* |
| christian | *chrestien* |
| christian purity | *virginitét* |
| city | *cit, citet* |
| clerk | *clerc, clerge* |
| clever | *cointe, saige, saive* |
| close | *pres, privez* |
| close to | *pres de* |
| closed | *ferma* |
| clothes | *despueille, dras* |
| come | *kar, venez, venir* |
| come out | *issir* |
| comes | *vendra* |
| comfort | *cunfort* |
| coming | *venir* |
| commanded | *comandé* |
| commit | *engagier, mustra* |
| commit a crime | *mesprendre* |
| committed | *forfait* |

| English | Old French |
|---|---|
| companions | *cumpaignuns* |
| compared with | *contre* |
| complain | *plaindre* |
| completely | *tot* |
| composed | *fez* |
| conceal | *celer* |
| concealed | *cela* |
| concern | *chaloir* |
| condition | *estre* |
| confess | *clamer* |
| conquer | *conquerre, cunquerre, veintre* |
| consider | *tenir* |
| consolation | *consolation* |
| conversation | *parlement* |
| cook | *cuire* |
| could | *avreie, peüst, poeit, pot pout, puis* |
| could-have | *pis?* |
| could-they | *porent* |
| counsel | *cunseil* |
| counselled | *cunseilla* |
| counsellor | *conseilleor, conseillier* |
| count | *conte, conter* |
| country | *cuntree, païs, regne, terre* |
| court | *curt* |
| courted | *preiee* |
| courteous | *curteis* |
| cowardly | *recreant* |
| craft | *art* |
| crazy | *fol* |
| creature | *chose, cose, ren, rien* |
| crimson | *vermeille* |
| crippled | *enferm* |
| cross | *trespasser* |
| cruel | *dur* |
| cry | *plorer* |
| cry out | *escrier* |
| cut | *trenchier* |
| cut off | *tolir* |

# D, d

| English | Old French |
|---|---|
| dame | *dame* |

| English | Old French | English | Old French |
|---|---|---|---|
| danger | *peril* | distaff | *queloigne, quenoille* |
| dare | *osasse, oser* | distress | *destresce, ire* |
| dark | *have* | distressed | *iré, irié* |
| daughter | *fille* | do | *faire* |
| day | *di, jor, jorn* | do nothing | *feindre* |
| days | *jurs* | does | *fait* |
| day's journey | *jornee* | dogs | *chien, chiens* |
| days-passed | *Jadis* | doing | *fereit* |
| dear | *bel* | done | *faire, fait, faites* |
| death | *mort* | do-not | *nen, n'en* |
| deceit | *feintise* | doors | *hus* |
| deceive | *deçoivre, engeignier, engignier* | doubt | *doter, duter, dutez* |
| | | dove | *colomb, colon* |
| decorative object | *garnement* | draws | *trait* |
| dedicated | *duné* | dread | *redut* |
| deep | *altain* | dressed | *aturnez, vestuz* |
| defeat | *desconfire* | drew-close | *traist* |
| defense | *garant, garent, resort* | drink | *abevrez, bevre* |
| deign | *daignier* | dug-out | *cavee* |
| delay | *demoree, respit* | duke | *duc* |
| delicious | *delicios* | dwelling | *ostel* |
| demeanour | *contenant* | | |
| demolish | *desconfire* | | |
| demon | *malfé* | | |

# E, e

| English | Old French | English | Old French |
|---|---|---|---|
| deny | *mentir, renier, renoier* | earlier | *ainc, ains, ainz* |
| departed | *departi* | earth | *terre* |
| deprive | *conserrer, consirrer* | earthly life | *secle, seule, siecle* |
| descend | *descendre* | eat | *mangier, manjuer* |
| desire | *faim* | educated | *saige, saive* |
| desired | *requise* | eight | *huit* |
| destroy | *abatre, perdrai, perir* | elegant | *cointe* |
| destruction | *perte* | ell | *alne* |
| devil | *deable, diavle, enemi, malfé* | embraces | *l'acole* |
| | | emperor | *empereor* |
| devotion | *servise* | empty | *vain, vuide, vuit* |
| devour | *devorer* | encountered | *encuntré* |
| devours | *devure* | end | *fenir, finir* |
| did-he | *s'en* | enemy | *enemi* |
| die | *morir* | energy | *element* |
| difficulty | *destreit* | engaging | *frans* |
| direct | *droit* | enraged | *enragiez* |
| direction | *sen, sens* | entered | *entrerent* |
| disaster | *mal* | entire | *entier, entiers* |
| disgrace | *aviler, honte* | entirely | *tot* |
| dismembered | *depescié* | escort | *convoier* |
| dismount | *descendre* | | |

| English | Old French | English | Old French |
|---------|-----------|---------|-----------|
| esteem | anor, enor, onor, prisier, proisier | few | pau, poi, pou |
| event | cas | fewer | mains, meins, moins |
| ever | ja, onques | fief | anor, chasez, enor, onor |
| every | tot | fierce | fier, fort |
| everyone | Ceo | fifteen | quinze |
| evil | mal | find | trover |
| except | fors, hors | finery | parament |
| excessively | trop | finger | dei, doi |
| exhausted | mat, recreant | fire | feu, fou |
| exhort | enorter | first | premiers, primes |
| expedition | chevauchie | flee from | fuier, fuir |
| expensive | cher, riche | flesh | char, charn |
| explaine | demostrer | flower | flor, florir |
| expression | contenant | fly | voler |
| extremely | trop | folding chair for important person | faldestoed, faldestuef, faldestuel |
| eye | oeuil, oil | followed | siwant |
| | | fondness | chierté |
| | | food | peüz |
| **F, f** | | foot | pié |
| | | for | car, por, pur, quar, que, sa |
| face | vis, visage | for a long time | longement |
| face downwards | adenz | for the sake of | anpur, enpur |
| facility | aise | forbid | veer |
| fail | mentir | force | element |
| faint | se pasmer | forehead | temple |
| fair | gent | forest | bois, bos, forest, gualdine |
| faith | fei, foi | forests | forez |
| fall | cas, chaeir, cheoir, perte | forget | ubliër |
| false | | forgive | pardoner |
| false | | for-him | celui |
| family | feu, fou, lignage, parage | form | figure |
| far | loin, loing, lonc, long, luin | formerly | ça en arriere |
| far away | loin, loing, lonc, luin | for-the-love-of | s'amur |
| father | parent, pere | forward | avant |
| favor | servise | found | trovez |
| fear | criem, esfrei, paor, peor, poür, redoter | found-out | sot |
| feeble | mat | frequently | avenir, sovent |
| feed | paistre, pestre | friend | ami, amie, amis |
| feel | sentir | friendship | amistié |
| feet | pié | frightened | esbai |
| felony | felunie | from | de, del |
| fence | escremir, escrimer | from the direction of | de vers, devers |

| English | Old French | English | Old French |
|---|---|---|---|
| from-me | *mei* | grant | *creanter, durrai, granter, otrei, otrier, otroier* |
| full | *plain, plein, ses* | grass | *erbre* |
| full of fervor | *balt* | great | *grant, magne* |
| full of joy | *joieus* | greatly | *durement, forment* |
| furious | *enragié, iré, irié* | Greek | *gré, gri, grieu, griu* |
| further | *mais* | green | *vert* |
| furthermore | *mes* | greet | *saluer* |
| | | grief | *dol, duel, ennui* |
| | | grow | *creistre, croistre* |

# G, g

| | | grow worse | *angregier* |
|---|---|---|---|
| | | guard | *garder, guardent* |
| | | guarded | *guarderent* |
| game | *table* | | |
| garden | *vergier* | | |
| Garulf | *Garulf* | | |

# H, h

| gave | *duna* | | |
|---|---|---|---|
| generous | *riche* | | |
| gentle | *bealz, dolz, dous* | ha | *ha* |
| gentleman | *chevaliers* | had | *a, aveit, deüst, fet, fust, la, l'aveit, l'orent, ot, tel, tindrent* |
| girl | *polle, pucele* | | |
| girl of noble birth | *damoiselle* | | |
| give | *baillier, comander, doner, rendre* | had-been | *fusse* |
| | | handsome | *Beals, bel, gent* |
| give in | *concreidre* | hang | *pendre* |
| given | *doner* | happen | *avenir* |
| gladly | *volentiers* | happened | *avenue, avint, fu, issi* |
| glory | *gloire* | happy | *balt, lié, liet, liez* |
| glove | *gant* | harbour | *port* |
| go | *aler, alez, en, met, venir, vois* | hard | *dur, durement, fort* |
| | | harm | *damage, foler, laid, mal, mesfacent, tucha* |
| go away | *se departir* | | |
| go by | *trespasser* | has | *a, l'ait, tel* |
| go out | *issir* | has-done | *fait* |
| go to the help of | *secorer* | has-it | *fist* |
| god | *deu, element* | hasten | *se hasteier, se haster* |
| god's | *deu* | hated | *haï* |
| godson | *filuel* | hates | *het* |
| goes | *vait, vet* | hatred | *haine* |
| gold | *or* | hauberk | *halberc, osberc* |
| gone | *alé, alez* | have | *ai, aveir, avoir, avrez, tenir* |
| good | *ben, bien, bon, bons* | | |
| good fortune | *ben, bien* | have back | *ravoir* |
| grace | *clementiam, merci, pardon* | have to | *devoir* |
| | | have-we | *avum* |
| grand | *granz* | he | *a, cil, el, Ele, en, est, hum, i, Il, le, li, lui, mes, ne, quis, se* |
| grandson | *neveu, nevot* | | |

| English | Old French | English | Old French |
|---------|-----------|---------|-----------|
| head | *chief, teste* | horror | *poür, tristece* |
| health | *santé* | hour | *eure, ore* |
| hear | *entendre, odir, Oëz, oir, oïr* | house | *maison, maisun, ostel* |
| | | household | *maisnie, maisniee* |
| heard | *entendu, oï* | how | *coment, cum, sa* |
| heart | *coer, cor, cors, cuer, curage* | hunger | *faim* |
| | | hunt | *chacier, chasser* |
| heathen | *pagien, paien* | hunters | *veneür* |
| heaven | *ciel* | hurry | *Espleitiez* |
| he-called | *apela* | husband | *seignur, sire* |
| he-embraced | *l'acola* | | |
| he-had | *aveit, furent* | | |
| held | *tens, tint* | | |
| hell | *enfern* | | |

## I, i

| English | Old French | English | Old French |
|---------|-----------|---------|-----------|
| hello | *ha* | i | *i, jeo, jes, jeu, jo, jol, jou, me* |
| help | *sucurs* | | |
| he-perceived | *s'aparceit* | i-am | *sui* |
| her | *la, Le, l'en, li, sis, sun* | i-begin | *m'entremet* |
| here | *ça, çai, ci, ici, issi* | if | *se, s'en, si* |
| her-had | *l'aveit* | if-he | *S'il* |
| he-runs | *curut* | if-him | *s'il* |
| he-stayed | *herberja* | if-she | *s'el* |
| he-wanted | *volentiers* | if-some | *s'alcune* |
| he-was | *esteit* | ignorance | *nonsavoir* |
| he-went | *ala, alout* | i-hear | *oï* |
| high | *alt, altain, aut, halt* | i-know | *sai* |
| hill | *pui* | ill | *enferm* |
| him | *cil, hum, ki, le, l'en, li, l'i, lui* | illness | *enfermeté, mal* |
| | | immediately | *endreit, maintenant, sempre, sempres, tantost, tost* |
| him-had | *l'aveit* | | |
| him-loved | *l'amout* | | |
| himself | *meïsmes* | important | *alt, aut, halt* |
| his | *la, le, les, li, sa, ses, soens, son, sun* | in | *a, ad, Al, as, El, en, sun* |
| | | in front of | *devant* |
| his-adventure | *s'aventure* | in here | *ceanz, seans* |
| hit | *fiere* | in order that | *com, cum* |
| hither | *ça, çai* | in the direction of | *de vers, devers* |
| hold | *tenir* | in the middle | *par mi, parmi* |
| hollow | *cruese* | in the midst of | *entre* |
| holy | *saint* | in the presence of | *devant* |
| home | *maisun* | in vain | *mar* |
| homes | *maisun* | indeed | *ja, voir* |
| honor | *anor, enor, fei, foi, honestét, onor* | indicate | *demostrer* |
| | | indicated | *enseigna* |
| honored | *honore* | inform | *enseignier* |
| horn | *cor, corn* | inquired | *enquis* |

| English | Old French |
|---|---|
| inside | *dedenz* |
| in-such-way | *cumfaitement* |
| intention | *maniere* |
| in-those | *es* |
| into | *en* |
| invent | *engeignier, engignier* |
| inventory | *livre* |
| invoke | *reclamer* |
| iron | *fer* |
| is | *a, en, est, fu, i, la, m'est, s'est* |
| is-humbled | *s'umilie* |
| island | *ille, isle* |
| it | *ce, ceo, ceu, ço, il, la, le, s'en* |
| it-is | *c'est* |
| it-seems | *esciënt* |
| i-understand | *j'entent* |
| ivory horn | *olifant* |
| i-want | *vueil* |
| i-wish | *vueil, vus* |
| I-would-be | *sereie* |

# J, j

| English | Old French |
|---|---|
| jest | *gab* |
| joy | *joi, joie* |
| joyful | *lié, liet* |
| joyous | *joius* |
| just | *or* |

# K, k

| English | Old French |
|---|---|
| keep | *tenir* |
| keep from | *astenir* |
| kill | *morir, ocire* |
| king | *regem, rei, reis, roi* |
| kingdom | *regne* |
| king's | *rei* |
| kiss | *baisier* |
| kissed | *baisa* |
| kisses | *baise* |
| knew | *saveit, seümes, sout* |
| knight | *chevalier, chevaliers* |
| knights | *chevaliers* |
| knock down | *abatre* |
| know | *apercevoir, savez, savoir* |
| knowing | *saveit* |
| knowledge | *escïent* |
| known | *cuneüz, seü* |
| known-him | *veü* |
| knows | *set* |

# L, l

| English | Old French |
|---|---|
| lady | *dame* |
| lament | *se dementer* |
| land | *terre* |
| large | *grant* |
| lay | *lais* |
| lay siege | *asseoir* |
| lays | *lais* |
| lead | *deduire, mener* |
| leave | *congié, cungié, guerpir, laissier, se departir* |
| led-himself | *cunteneit* |
| left | *laissier* |
| leg | *jambe* |
| legitimate | *leal, loial* |
| lend | *prester* |
| less | *mains, meins, moins* |
| lesson | *moralité* |
| let | *fai, laissier, les, lur* |
| letter | *chartre* |
| let-us | *Alum* |
| let-us-leave | *laissuns* |
| liberal art | *art* |
| lie | *favele, gesir, mentir* |
| lie down | *couchier, se coucher* |
| life | *estre* |
| lift up | *lever* |
| light | *legier, ligier, loigier* |
| light-hearted | *legier, ligier, loigier* |
| likewise | *aussi* |
| lily | *lil* |
| lineage | *lignage* |
| listen | *entent, Oëz* |
| listen to | *escolter* |

| English | Old French | English | Old French |
|---|---|---|---|
| little | *pau, petit, poi, pou* | mass | *masse* |
| live | *deduire, vif* | matter | *afaire, chaloir* |
| lived | *maneit* | matting | *nate* |
| lodge | *herbergier* | me | *jo, me, mei, mes* |
| long | *loing, lonc, long, longement, lung, lungement* | mean | *mal* |
| | | meat | *char, charn* |
| long-after | *lungement* | meet | *assanler, assembler, encontrer* |
| look at | *aviser* | meeting | *parlement* |
| look for | *quere, querre* | melody | *chant* |
| look-at | *esguardez* | men | *humes* |
| loot | *eschec* | menace | *manace, menace* |
| lord | *dam, dan, seignor, seignur* | mercy | *merci* |
| | | message | *message* |
| lose | *perdre* | messenger | *message* |
| loss | *perdre* | might | *vertu* |
| lost | *perdeit, perduz* | mile | *liue, live* |
| love | *amer, amor, chier, eim, s'amur* | mine | *mei* |
| | | miracle | *miracle* |
| loved | *amé, amee, amez, amot, chier* | misdeed | *mesfaire* |
| | | miserable | *chaitif* |
| lover | *amant* | misery | *poverté* |
| loyal | *leal, loial* | misguided | *meserrez* |
| | | mislead | *deçoivre* |

# M, m

| | | missed | *perdeit* |
|---|---|---|---|
| | | mistake | *colpe, cope, corpe, pechié, tort* |
| madam | *Dame* | mistreatment | *mesfait* |
| made | *faire, faiseit* | mistress | *drue* |
| maiden | *pucele* | money | *argent* |
| make | *faire, faites* | monk | *moine, monie* |
| make a mistake | *mesprendre* | more | *mais, mes, plus, plusur, remest* |
| make known | *reveler* | | |
| makes | *Faites* | most | *Mult, plus* |
| man | *home, huem, hume, ome* | mother | *mere* |
| | | mountain | *mont, montaigne, pui* |
| manifest | *apert* | mourn | *plaindre* |
| manner | *guise* | mouth | *bouche, buche* |
| many | *asez, assés, bien, maint, meinte, molt, mout, mult, plusur, plusurs, sovent* | much | *Asez, assés, bien, guaires, molt, mout, mult, tel, tres* |
| many a | *maint* | my | *ma, Mes, mon, mun* |
| married | *espusee* | my-heart | *cuer* |
| marry | *esposer* | my-lord | *Sire* |
| marvel | *merveille* | my-love | *m'amur* |
| marvellously | *merveille* | myself | *meïsmes* |

| English | Old French |
|---|---|
| **N, n** | |
| name | *nom, nomer, non* |
| naught | *ne* |
| near | *lez* |
| neighbours | *veisins* |
| nephew | *neveu, nevot* |
| never | *Ja, nonque, unc, unkes* |
| never-will | *n'i* |
| next to | *dales, dallĂŠ, dalles* |
| next to; beside | *delé, deleiz, deles* |
| next-to | *s'alout* |
| night | *nuit* |
| no | *ne, nul, nule* |
| noble | *debonaire, esteit, gentil* |
| nobly | *noblement* |
| noise | *estor, estorm, vois, voiz* |
| no-longer | *ne* |
| none | *ne, n'i, nuls* |
| No-one | *N'i* |
| nor | *ne, nel, n'en, ni* |
| Normans | *Norman* |
| nose | *nes* |
| noselessly | *esnasees* |
| noses | *nes* |
| not | *enne, mie, ne, Nel, nen, n'en, non, nule, pas* |
| not any | *nul* |
| not at all | *nïent* |
| not-at-all | *mie* |
| not-had | *n'out* |
| not-has | *n'a* |
| nothing | *feiz, nïënt, rien, rien?* |
| notice | *apercevoir* |
| noticed | *l'aperceut* |
| not-is | *n'est* |
| now | *Ja, jai, or, ore* |
| nude | *nuz* |
| **O, o** | |
| oath | *sairement* |
| observe | *viseter* |

| English | Old French |
|---|---|
| octave | *huitaves* |
| of | *a, al, ala, De, del, des, e, ki, la, ot, se* |
| of it | *en* |
| of noble lineage | *emparenté* |
| of the king | *regal* |
| of which | *dont, dunt* |
| of whom | *dont, dunt* |
| of-a-man | *d'ume* |
| offer | *presenter* |
| of-him | *l'ai, qu'um* |
| of-one | *d'une* |
| often | *sovent* |
| of-the | *ala* |
| of-them | *des* |
| of-this | *del* |
| old | *veil, vieil, viez* |
| on | *a, ad, en, seur, sor, soure, Sur* |
| on top of | *en* |
| once | *onques* |
| one | *le, om, on, un, Une, uns* |
| open | *apert* |
| oppose | *contredire* |
| opposition | *cuntredit* |
| or | *o, u* |
| orchard | *vergier* |
| order | *comander, rover* |
| ordered | *mandez* |
| origin | *parage* |
| other | *altre* |
| our | *nostre* |
| out | *fors, hors* |
| out of | *hors* |
| out-of | *de* |
| outside | *fors* |
| over | *seur, sor, soure, sur* |
| overcome | *veintre* |
| overcome completely | *tresprendre* |
| overload | *encombrer* |
| owe | *dei* |
| own | *baillier, demeine* |
| **P, p** | |

47

| English | Old French | English | Old French |
|---|---|---|---|
| pagan | pagien, paien | precisely | endreit |
| page | bacheler, bachelor | prepare | atorner |
| pain | dolor, dolur, enoi, enui | present | porofrir, present, presenter |
| pardon | pardoner | | |
| parent | parent | presently | ore |
| part | part, partez, piece | pretense | feintise |
| part-with | partir | previously | suliëz |
| party | feste | prison | piere, pierre, prison, serre |
| pass | trespasser | | |
| path | chemin, sentier | prize | pris |
| pay | prist | proclaim | clamer |
| pay attention | entendre, penser | profession | menestier |
| pay attention to | escolter | promise | acreanter, fiance |
| peace | pes | proper | droit |
| people | gent, suens | prosecute | asproier |
| period | terme | protection | garant, garent |
| period of time | terme, termine | protrude | empeindre |
| perish | perdre, perir | proud | fier |
| permission | congié, pardon | pull | tirer |
| permission to leave | congié | pure | mer, mier |
| persecution | empedement | purposed | purpensa |
| person | figure, ren, rien | pursue | porchacier |
| physical or moral weakness | enfermeté | purveyor | porveor |
| | | put | feiz, mectre, met, metre, mettre |
| piece | piece | | |
| pigeon | colomb, colon | puts | met |
| pine tree | pin | | |
| pity | merci | | |
| place | asseoir, metez | | |

# Q, q

| English | Old French |
|---|---|
| queen | raine, reine, roine |
| queried | enquis |
| questioned | mise |
| questions | demanda |
| quickly | menu, menut, tost |

| play | joer |
|---|---|
| please | plaire |
| plunder | preie |
| point out | enseignier |
| poor | povre |
| port | port |
| portion | part |
| poverty | poverté |
| power | vertu |

# R, r

| English | Old French |
|---|---|
| race | gent |
| rage | rage |
| ran | curut |
| rank | parage |
| rather | ainc, ains, ainz, mais, mels, miels |
| reach | ataindre |
| real | verai |

| powerful | riche |
|---|---|
| praise | loër |
| praised | losenja |
| pray | orer, preier, prier |
| prayer | oraison, orison, priement |
| precious cloth | paile |
| precious object | parament |

| English | Old French | English | Old French |
|---------|-----------|---------|-----------|
| really | bien, voirement | ride | chevauchie |
| reason | entente, raison, raisun | right | droit, endreit |
| receive | baillier | ring | anel |
| receive as guest | herbergier | road | veie |
| receives | prent | room | chambre |
| recognize | aviser, reconoistre | rooms | chambres |
| recommend | comander | rose | rose |
| recounted | cunta, cunté | royal | regal |
| re-dress | reveste | royal apartment | chambre |
| refined | cointe | ruin | eissil, essil, issil |
| refuse | veer | run | corre |
| refuse to believe | mescroire | running | curut |
| regain | ataindre | | |
| regret | plaindre | | |
| reject | geter, giter | | |
| rejoice | esleecier | | |
| relate | conter | | |
| released | descuplé | | |
| relieved | guarie | | |
| remain | demorer, ester, maindre, remanoir | | |
| remained | remest | | |
| remains | relef | | |
| remedy | resort | | |
| remember | resovenir | | |
| rememberance | remembrance | | |
| repair | refaire | | |
| repeatedly | Suventes | | |
| resign | conserrer, consirrer | | |
| resist | contredire, remanoir | | |
| respect | anor, enor, onor | | |
| responded | respunt | | |
| rest | se reposer | | |
| restriction | resort | | |
| retained | retenu | | |
| retain-him | retenir | | |
| return | rendre, retor, retorn, revienc, torner | | |
| returned | rendi, rendu, repaira, repairiez, turnez | | |
| reveal | reveler | | |
| revealed | descovri | | |
| revolt | reveler | | |
| reward | guerredoner | | |
| riches | argent | | |
| richly | richement | | |

# S, s

| English | Old French |
|---------|-----------|
| sad | mat |
| sadness | tristece |
| said | diënt, dist, fait, fet |
| salute | saluer |
| savage | salvage |
| saw | choisi, veïst, vit |
| say | dire |
| scraps | relef |
| sea | mer |
| seduce | engeignier, engignier, enorter |
| see | aviser, veoir |
| seek | porchacier |
| seen | veü |
| sees | veit |
| segment | piece |
| seize | prendre, tenir |
| seized | pris, prist |
| sense | sen, sens |
| sent-for | manda |
| servant | pucele, servant |
| serve | servir |
| served | servir |
| service | menestier, servise |
| set | mise |
| set up | asseoir |
| seven | set |
| several | pluisor, plusor |
| shame | honte, hunte |
| she | el, ele, li, se |

| English | Old French | English | Old French |
|---|---|---|---|
| shed tears | *plorer* | soul | *alme, ame, anima, anme, arme* |
| she-dressed | *s'apareillot* | sound | *soner, suner* |
| shelter | *herbergier* | speak | *parler* |
| she-sent-for | *l'enveia* | speech | *oraison, orison, parole, raison* |
| she-was-terrified | *s'esfrea* | spin | *filer* |
| shield | *escu* | spiritual purity | *virginitét* |
| ship | *nef* | staircase | *degré* |
| should | *devez* | stake | *ré, rei, rez* |
| shout | *braire, crier, escrier* | stand | *ester, estut* |
| show | *demostrer, mener* | standard bearer | *gunfanuner* |
| shy away | *feindre* | standing | *estait* |
| sick | *have* | start | *comencier* |
| sides | *parz* | stay | *demoree, demorer, maindre, remanoir* |
| sight | *ses* | stayed | *esteit* |
| silver | *argent* | stick | *verge* |
| simple bed | *grabatum* | still | *encor, encore, uncore* |
| sin | *colpe, cope, corpe, pechié* | stirrup | *estrié* |
| since | *puis* | stomach | *pance* |
| sing | *braire, chanter* | stone | *piere, pierre* |
| sir | *dam, dan* | stop | *fenir, finir* |
| sire | *Sire* | story | *favele* |
| sires | *Seignur* | straight | *dreit* |
| sit | *seoir* | street | *rue* |
| skill | *engien, engin* | strength | *vertu* |
| sleep | *som, some* | striving | *travailliez* |
| sleeping | *dormant* | strong | *alt, aut, fier, fort, halt, riche* |
| slept | *culchier* | study | *estude, estudie* |
| small | *petit* | subsequently | *end, ent, puis* |
| smash to pieces | *pecier* | such | *cele, ceo, tant, tel* |
| smell | *sentir* | such-time | *tant* |
| snatched | *esracha* | suffer | *pener* |
| so | *dunc, fu, Issi, si, Tant, vis* | suffering | *dol, dolor, duel, paine, peine* |
| so much | *tant* | summon | *apeler* |
| somber | *have* | supple | *legier, ligier, loigier* |
| some | *alkun, aucun* | support | *sostenir* |
| somebody | *alme, ame, anme, arme* | sure | *seur, sur* |
| somehow | *coment* | surprised | *esbai* |
| so-much | *tant* | suspect | *mescroire* |
| son | *fil, filuel* | sustain | *sostenir* |
| song | *chant* | sweet | *debonaire, dolz, dous, dulz* |
| soon | *maintenant, tost* | swift | *hastif* |
| sorely | *durement* | | |
| sorrowful | *dolent* | | |
| sought-for | *demandez* | | |

| English | Old French |
|---|---|
| swoon | *se pasmer* |
| sword | *espee* |

# T, t

| English | Old French |
|---|---|
| table | *table* |
| take | *mener, prendre* |
| take hold of | *prendre* |
| take off | *tolir* |
| take-care | *guardez* |
| taken-aside | *prise* |
| taken-away | *toli* |
| takes | *meine* |
| talk | *parler* |
| tall | *grant* |
| task | *servise* |
| teach | *enseignier* |
| tear | *deciré* |
| teeth | *denz* |
| tell | *di, dire, dis, dist, dites, noncier* |
| tells | *direit* |
| temple | *temple* |
| tenderly | *tendrement* |
| term | *terme* |
| territory | *chambre* |
| than | *de, que* |
| thanks | *mercie* |
| that | *a, ce, cele, ceo, ceu, cil, ço, e, est, ki, la, l'a, qu'a, que, qui, qu'il, tant* |
| that much | *si* |
| that way | *si* |
| that-day | *jur* |
| that-heard | *l'oï* |
| that-in | *qu'en* |
| that-one | *celui* |
| that-time | *cele* |
| the | *al, as, cel, la, le, les, li* |
| the-adventure | *l'aventure* |
| the-beast | *beste* |
| the-clothing | *despueille* |
| the-country | *païs* |
| the-end | *chief* |
| the-event | *l'aventure* |

| English | Old French |
|---|---|
| theft | *ravine* |
| their | *leur, lor, lur* |
| the-king | *rei* |
| the-knight | *chevalier* |
| the-last | *Cist* |
| the-morning | *demain* |
| then | *a, donc, en, puis, s'en, unt* |
| the-name | *nun* |
| the-one | *Cil* |
| the-other | *l'altre* |
| the-palace | *palais* |
| there | *i, ilec, iluec, iluoc, La, l'en, vet* |
| therefore | *donc, Kar, Pur* |
| these | *cez* |
| the-story | *L'aventure* |
| the-time | *piece* |
| the-wife | *femme* |
| they | *Cil, il, l'unt, sunt, unt* |
| they-call | *l'apelent* |
| they-find | *truevent* |
| they-had | *eüz* |
| they-live | *viveient* |
| they-were | *sunt* |
| they-would-have | *l'eüssent* |
| thick | *espés* |
| thing | *chose, cose, ren, rien* |
| think | *cuidier, penser* |
| thirty four | *trente et quatre* |
| this | *ce, cele, ceo, Cest, ceste, ceu, cist, ço, euc, Iceste, l'a, le, li, o, ou, sa* |
| this-day | *hui* |
| this-he | *Cil* |
| those | *cels* |
| thought | *quidot* |
| thought-they | *quidouent* |
| thousand | *millier* |
| threatened | *manaça, manacié* |
| three | *trei, treis, trois* |
| throne | *faldestoed, faldestuef, faldestuel* |
| through | *par, par mi, parmi* |
| throw | *geter, giter* |

| English | Old French | English | Old French |
|---|---|---|---|
| thus | *Issi, si, s'i* | trouble | *damage, guerre* |
| time | *eure, feiz, ore, tans, tens, veiz* | troubled | *esbai* |
| | | true | *verai* |
| times | *feiz* | true | *veraie* |
| time-to-time | *sovent* | true | *veritez* |
| title | *nom, non* | true | *voir* |
| to | *a, ad, al, de, del, en, encontre, se, seur, sor, soure, sur, vers* | truly | *voir* |
| | | try | *entendre* |
| | | tumult | *estor, estorm* |
| to-ask | *demandasse* | turn | *atorner, torner* |
| to-be | *seit* | two | *Dous* |
| to-bite | *mordre* | | |
| today | *oi, ue, ui* | | |
| to-embrace | *enbracier* | | |
| together | *comunalment, ensemble* | | |

# U, u

| English | Old French | English | Old French |
|---|---|---|---|
| together with | *ensemble od* | ugly | *vilain* |
| to-go | *errer* | under | *a, desos, desous, sos, soz, suz* |
| to-help | *aidier* | | |
| to-him | *ariere, li* | under-pressed | *suzprist* |
| to-lie | *gisir* | understand | *entendre* |
| to-lose | *perduz* | understanding | *sages* |
| to-me | *me, mei, m'en, Mun* | unhappy person | *entrepris* |
| too much | *trop* | unhealthy | *enferm* |
| took | *mena, menez, pris, toluz* | unrefined | *dur* |
| | | until | *desi, tant, tresqu', trusqu'* |
| to-part | *partir* | | |
| to-recount | *cunter* | until now | *ça en arriere* |
| torment | *asproier, enoi, enui, paine, peine* | unto | *En* |
| | | up | *sus, suz* |
| torture | *pener* | up to | *a, ad, jusqu'a, tresqu', trusqu'* |
| to-separate | *desevrer* | | |
| to-talk-with | *parler* | urge | *enorter* |
| totally | *tuz* | us | *nus* |
| to-the | *al, la* | used | *suleit* |
| tourney | *tornoier* | utter | *geter, giter, soner, suner* |
| toward | *vers* | | |
| towards | *encontre, envers, vers* | | |
| tower | *tor* | | |

# V, v

| English | Old French | English | Old French |
|---|---|---|---|
| town | *cit, citet* | valiant | *vaillant* |
| travelled | *tint* | vanquish | *veintre* |
| travels | *tint* | various | *divers* |
| treated | *bailliz, mis* | very | *durement, forment, molt, mout, Mult, tres forment* |
| tree | *bois, bos* | | |
| tremble | *trembler* | | |
| troops | *compaigne* | very much | |
| | | very well | *asez, assés* |

| English | Old French | English | Old French |
|---|---|---|---|
| very-important | *munte* | which | *dunt, ki, qu'avez, que, quel, qu'il* |
| very-well | *bonement, tresbien* | which-of | *qu'il* |
| village | *rue* | which-that | *qu'il* |
| virgin | *virge* | whirl around | *tornoier* |
| visible | *aparant, apert* | white | *blanc* |
| visit | *viseter* | who | *ki, le, que, qui, s'en* |
| voice | *vois, voiz* | who-here | *qu'ici* |
| | | who-him | *celui* |
| | | whole | *tot* |
| | | whose | *dont, dunt* |

# W, w

| English | Old French | English | Old French |
|---|---|---|---|
| | | wide | *lee* |
| wall | *mur* | wife | *espuse, femme* |
| want | *quere, querre, voloir, vueil, vueille* | wild rose | *aiglantier, aiglent* |
| wanted | *voleit, volt* | will-do | *ferez* |
| wants | *volt* | willed | *volt* |
| war | *guerre* | will-hunt | *chacerai* |
| war cry | *enseigne* | willing | *volentiers* |
| was | *a, ert, est, esté, ester, fu, fust, li, s'en* | will-part | *partirai* |
| | | will-tell | *dirai* |
| was-he | *esteit* | wine | *vin* |
| watch over | *garder* | wise | *sages* |
| way | *guise, maniere, veie* | with | *atot, avec, avoc, avuec, cum, de, en, ensemble, i, mes, o, od, of, ot, qu'el* |
| way of life | *estre* | | |
| ways | *endreit* | | |
| we | *nos, nus* | | |
| weak | *enferm, vain* | with-a | *d'une* |
| weapon | *fer* | without | *senz* |
| wear | *porter* | woman | *dame, Femme* |
| weather | *tans, tens* | women | *femmes* |
| week | *semeine* | wonder | *merveille* |
| well | *bel, bien* | wonders | *merveille* |
| well-being | *ben, bien, santé* | woods | *boscages* |
| went | *ala, alez, alout, repairié, vait, vers* | word | *mot, parlement, parole, raison, vois, voiz* |
| were | *eüsse, furent* | world | *mund, secle, seule, siecle* |
| werewolf | *Bisclavret* | | |
| wetched | *dolent* | worse | *peüst* |
| we-will-see | *verruns* | worship | *adurer* |
| what | *cument, que, quei, quel, qu'est, qui, qu'il* | worthy-man | *prozdum* |
| | | would | *deüst* |
| what is surprising | *merveille* | would-be | *fussent* |
| what-have | *Qu'ai* | would-have | *eüst* |
| when | *com, comme, Quant, que* | would-look-like | *semblereit* |
| | | wretched | *mal* |
| where | *ou, u* | wretchedness | *eissil, essil, issil* |
| whether | *s'il, U* | | |

| English | Old French |
|---|---|
| wrongly | *mar* |

# Y, y

| | |
|---|---|
| year | *an* |
| yet | *encor, encore, si, uncore* |
| yield | *ploier* |
| you | *die, Ne, tu, vos, vus* |
| you-have | *vus* |
| you-heard | *oïe* |
| young knight aspirant | *bacheler, bachelor* |
| young man | *bacheler, bachelor* |
| your | *tes, ton, vostre, voz, vus* |
| yours | *vus* |
| you-see | *vei* |

# Z, z

| | |
|---|---|
| zeal | *estude, estudie* |

Notes

Notes